W9-BNY-762

THE CHEYENNE POOL

Also by Lewis B. Patten

GUNS AT GRAY BUTTE
PROUDLY THEY DIE
GIANT ON HORSEBACK
THE ARROGANT GUNS
NO GOD IN SAGUARO
DEATH WAITED AT RIALTO CREEK
BONES OF THE BUFFALO
DEATH OF A GUNFIGHTER
THE RED SABBATH
THE YOUNGERMAN GUNS
POSSE FROM POISON CREEK
RED RUNS THE RIVER
A DEATH IN INDIAN WELLS
SHOWDOWN AT MESILLA
THE TRIAL OF JUDAS WILEY

THE CHEYENNE POOL

LEWIS B. PATTEN

West

DISCARDED

DOUBLEDAY & COMPANY, INC.
GARDEN CITY, NEW YORK
1972

All of the characters in this book are fictitious, and any resemblance to actual persons, living or dead, is purely coincidental.

First Edition

ISBN: 0-385-02262-X
Library of Congress Catalog Card Number 72–79415
Copyright © 1972 by Lewis B. Patten
All Rights Reserved
Printed in the United States of America

THE CHEYENNE POOL

CHAPTER 1

Dan Foxworthy swung from his horse, looped the reins around the tie-rail in front of the sheriff's office in Wootenburg and banged angrily inside. Ray Owens, the sheriff, glanced up, startled, from his desk. Foxworthy said intemperately, "You get your goddam horse and come with me!"

"Another cow?"

"Yes, by God, another cow! Shot through the neck!"

"You got a trail?"

"You're damned right I got a trail! Now quit asking stupid questions and get your horse!"

Owens's neck turned red but he didn't say anything. He got his hat, buckled on his holstered revolver and cartridge belt, and grabbed a rifle from the rack. He snatched his coat from the coat tree, shrugged into it, then dropped a handful of shells for the rifle into the side pocket. He followed Foxworthy into the street, turning and locking the door behind him.

The November wind, coming down off the snowy Continental Divide, was raw and cold. Owens buttoned his sheepskin coat and, head down, walked swiftly toward the livery barn a block and a half down the street.

Foxworthy untied his horse, mounted and followed at a walk. He was big, and solid, and as raw and intemperate as the wind howling down off the high divide. He was foreman of the Cheyenne Pool, a group that ran thirty thousand head of cattle on three hundred square miles of unfenced range. He was thirty-five years old.

Owens backed his horse out of his stall at the livery barn. The hostler, Pete Durfee, didn't even bother to come out of the warm tackroom and Owens didn't call for him. He saddled, pulled the cinch tight, swung to the horse's back and guided him across the hollow-sounding wooden floor to the big double doors. He rode down the ramp and out into the street, wondering uneasily if he shouldn't take time to round up a few men to help. Foxworthy's impatience decided him against the idea and he followed the Pool foreman out of town at a steady, mile-eating lope.

Foxworthy also wore a sheepskin coat and its bulkiness made him look even broader across the back. He seemed too big for the horse he rode. There was a rifle stock protruding from his saddle boot and the tip of his revolver holster showed below the skirt of his sheepskin coat.

They rode steadily northward, cutting straight across country now. The sky was a uniform steel gray. A flake of snow stung Owens's cheek, and another, and another still. He found himself hoping that snow would blot out the trail. If it did, a showdown could be postponed. He glanced hopefully toward the mountains. The clouds seemed too high and thin for heavy snow.

Foxworthy did not slacken his pace. He didn't look behind and he didn't talk. His back stayed stiff with anger as though he was deliberately keeping it alive.

Owens could understand that easily enough. Foxworthy was a cattleman. As a cattleman, he had a feeling for his stock. He might understand someone killing a young steer to eat. He might even understand rustling. But he couldn't understand the wantonness of this. The men who were killing cows were doing so only to get their unbranded calves, without the risk that cow and calf would pair up again and point the finger of guilt at the thief. The Cheyenne Pool lost both cow and calf. The thief only got the calf and usually a poor one at that, dropped late enough to have missed the spring branding, a calf that had somehow managed to escape branding during the summer months.

That happened, in spite of everything. In summer, the crew of the Cheyenne Pool was busy putting up hay for the winter months. They were busy digging out springs, fixing windmills and repairing tanks. They were riding line. It was inevitable that a good many calves were missed. A hundred or more, probably. And if the thieves killed every cow with an unbranded calf, it added up to a substantial loss.

An hour passed. The air, now, was filled with flakes of snow, driven almost horizontally on the wind. Owens kicked his horse and ranged up alongside Foxworthy. He yelled into the wind, "How much farther?"

"Five, six miles!"

"The snow's getting worse."

Foxworthy turned angry eyes on him. "You sure wish it would, don't you?"

Owens didn't answer. He let his horse drop back. Foxworthy was right. He had been wishing the snow would obliterate the trail.

The three hundred sections of range being used by the Cheyenne Pool were surrounded by grass-hungry ranchers who did not belong to the Pool. They knew the Pool had no legal right to hold that range and they wanted it.

So far they had held back, because they were not organized and because they were afraid. But if one of them was arrested for cattle theft . . . it might be the thing that would bring them together, that would bring their resistance to a head.

Dan Foxworthy did not agree with this point of view. To his direct way of thinking, a thief was a thief, and should be treated as such. He further believed that the way to stop rustling was to promptly catch and prosecute the rustlers.

There was already a slight accumulation of snow on the ground when they reached the body of the cow. She had obviously not been dead for more than a day, because she had not yet begun to bloat. But Owens didn't need more than a glance to know she had been suckling a calf. He saw the bullet wound in her neck and the blood that had run from it.

Foxworthy said, with smoldering anger, "Come on, let's go." He whirled his horse and spurred away. Despite the thin covering of snow on the ground, Owens was able to make out the tracks of a single horse. The horse had been dragging a calf. Sometimes he would see a place where the calf had balked and had been dragged bodily, sliding on all four feet. At one place he saw where the calf had fallen and been dragged ten feet or so before being allowed to get up again.

Foxworthy held his horse to a steady trot, eyes intent on the trail. The snow thickened and the wind began to die.

A mile from the place where they had found the body of the cow, Foxworthy hauled his horse to a sudden halt. He faced Owens and glared at him. "I can't follow it any .more. The snow's too deep."

Owens didn't know what to say. He knew almost anything he said would trigger an angry explosion from Foxworthy. He asked, "What now?"

Foxworthy had a strong face with a jutting chin, prom-

inent, high cheekbones, a hawklike nose below wide-spread, deep-set blue eyes. His face had lines in it, at the corners of the eyes and at both sides of the mouth. It was burned dark by sun and wind. When he laughed, which was seldom, he showed large, strong white teeth. He was a fine physical specimen, Owens thought, but he had no sympathy for weakness in anyone. Foxworthy's voice now came out like an angry gust of wind. "I'm not quitting, if that's what you mean. I've followed this damn trail far enough to know exactly where it's going to end."

Owens said, "Even if you find the calf, it won't do any good. Unless we trail it and prove that it's the one, there's not a damned thing I can do."

Foxworthy scowled, holding Owens's glance imperatively so that he couldn't look away. Owens said with his own defensive anger, "Damn it, don't look at me as if it was my fault! I didn't make it snow!"

"But you told me to come after you next time I found a cow so that you could take care of it legally."

"I'm still telling you. Sooner or later we'll find a trail we can follow. Sooner or later we'll catch up with them."

"And what will they get? Thirty days in jail? Or will they pack the jury with their friends and get clear away with it?"

"We won't know that until we try."

"Well, by God, I'm not going to wait!" Foxworthy turned his horse and rode away.

Owens kicked his own horse's sides and caught up. "Where are you going?"

"I know where this calf was taken and so do you. I'm going to drop in on the Stotts family."

"And what then?"

"I haven't decided yet."

Owens yelled, "I'm warning you . . ."

Foxworthy turned his head. His eyes still held anger, but now they held something else as well. Determination. He shouted back, "If you haven't got the stomach for it, then go on back to town!"

Stubbornly Owens kept pace. He didn't know what Foxworthy had in mind. What he did know was that he didn't dare go back.

At a steady lope, the pair swept along through the thickening snow toward the southern edge of the land held and claimed by the Cheyenne Pool. Sometimes, because of the terrain, Owens had to fall behind. But he never lost sight of the man ahead.

Stopping Foxworthy would be like trying to stop an avalanche. But maybe his presence with Foxworthy would prevent violence.

The southern boundary of the Cheyenne Pool range was the dry bed of Arapaho Creek. When they reached it, the snow was so thick that the far side was barely visible. But clustered there, on a bluff above the creek, Owens could see the haphazard collection of shacks in which the Stotts family lived.

Some were built of ties, stolen from the railroad, some of sod, some of lumber. Most had shingle roofs, on which the snow had been melted by the heat beneath. They were patched here and there with a straightened-out tin can, turned red by rust. There was no sign of activity in the yard, but smoke arose from several chimneys indicating the occupants were at home.

There was a fenced haystack near the corral. Cattle and horses were bunched hopefully against the fence on the lee side of the stack. Foxworthy rode his horse among these, paying particular attention to the half-dozen calves.

Apparently satisfied, he faced toward the house, with-

drew his rifle from the boot and fired it into the air. The report rolled flat across the land, dulled by the muffling effect of the falling snow. But it reached into the houses of the Stotts family. And it brought them piling out the doors, in various stages of undress, with guns clutched tightly in their hands.

Silence lay in the yard, unbroken even by a child's cry or the barking of a dog. Foxworthy's harsh voice cut through it like a knife. "I found another Pool cow shot half a dozen miles north of here."

Floyd Stotts, the oldest of the brothers, spoke up, hardly bothering to hide the half smile of triumph on his face. "What's that got to do with us? You sure as hell didn't trail the killer here. Not in this snow."

"I trailed him far enough!"

Owens wondered what Foxworthy was going to do. He didn't think the man would be rash enough to try shooting one of the Stotts men, not with all of them holding guns. But just in case, he shifted his position, unbuttoned his coat and shoved back the flap so that he could get at his gun if the need arose.

Floyd Stotts looked at him. "You going to arrest us, Ray? On evidence like that?"

Owens got no chance to reply. Foxworthy raised his rifle. Once more the report rolled flat across the land. Cattle and horses stampeded away from the stackyard fence, leaving one, a large weaner calf with a fresh brand lying dead in the falling snow.

Instantly Foxworthy swung the muzzle of his rifle toward the members of the Stotts family. Owens drew his own gun swiftly and instinctively. Foxworthy said in his harsh, intemperate voice, "Now! That's what's going to happen every goddam time I find a Cheyenne Pool cow shot. And it don't matter who got the calf, either. I'll shoot

one right here to make up for it." He let his stare bore into Floyd Stotts, whose face had lost all the color it had, as well as its triumphant smile. He said, "Want to take it up right now? You got a gun. Go right ahead."

Owens opened his mouth to speak, then shut it without saying anything. He knew his own intervention couldn't help and he also knew it might cause the situation to explode.

A minute dragged away. Foxworthy still held Floyd Stotts' glance with his own. He said, "We're leaving. Take a shot at us, and by God I'll come back here and burn every damn building you got clear down to the ground!"

He didn't look at the sheriff. He just turned his horse, presented his broad back to the Stotts family, and rode away.

Owens was ready, in case one of them raised a gun, but no one did. Foxworthy had, by now, disappeared into the snow. Owens turned and rode after him.

Behind him, only partly muffled by the snow, an uproar broke out. Women shrieked, and children cried. Men shouted and cursed angrily. Dogs began to bark.

Owens kicked his horse into a fast lope, following the trail left by Foxworthy in the snow. He caught up quickly because Foxworthy had held his own horse to a walk.

He reached out, overcome with fury, and seized the bridle of Foxworthy's horse. He raged, "Damn you, you didn't have to do that!"

"Somebody had to do something."

"What good do you think it's going to do?"

"I think it'll stop them from shootin' cows. Maybe not this time. But after they've lost half a dozen calves, they'll quit."

Owens released Foxworthy's horse. The Stotts family

was probably even now butchering the calf, so it wouldn't be a total loss. He said, "Next time they'll be waiting for you when you ride in."

"Then I'll take some men with me."

Owens stared at him helplessly. He said, "Damn it, don't you care? Don't you care what you've stirred up?"

"I didn't shoot that cow. I didn't start anything."

Their glances locked and it was Owens who looked away. He'd always liked Foxworthy before but now, suddenly, he found himself disliking the man. Shrugging lightly, he asked, "Where are you going now?"

"Home."

Home, for Foxworthy, was the bunkhouse at the Mathias ranch on Rustler Creek. That bunkhouse was headquarters for the Cheyenne Pool. The ranch itself, situated on a hundred and sixty acre homestead claim, was owned by Lutie Mathias, the twenty-two-year-old daughter of the late Hiram Mathias, who, with Colonel Ireland, had founded the Cheyenne Pool.

Owens growled, "You'd better grow eyes in the back of your head, that's all I've got to say. Because you'll need 'em before this is through."

Foxworthy didn't even bother to answer him. He touched his horse's sides with his spurs and rode away into the heavily falling snow. Owens stared after him helplessly.

CHAPTER 2

Riding north through the thickly falling flakes, it was as if Dan Foxworthy was riding in the clouds. The ground, covered with several inches of snow, was all but invisible and so was everything else. There were no landmarks with which to orient himself. But the horse knew where he was going, his instinct guiding him as unerringly as if he had been on a track.

Foxworthy rode with his head down, chin on chest, collar turned up against the wetness of the snow. Already there was an inch of it on his shoulders, hat, and back, but he didn't bother to brush it off. He seemed unaware of it.

Something back there in the yard of the Stotts' place had struck a responsive chord in his memory, and was deeply disturbing to him now. Frowning, he tried to figure out what it was.

He had been six when, in the year 1841, he had crossed the Missouri with his father and mother near Fort Leavenworth. They had settled illegally on Indian lands. At the end of the first year, still unmolested by Indians, they had a log cabin built, a garden that raised potatoes and vegetables for them to eat, and a smokehouse containing enough smoked venison to last the winter through.

The second year, his father had begun to clear the land, cutting trees, removing stumps. It was not until the third year that the first small patch of land was plowed and put into crops.

Dan Foxworthy had worked from the time he was old enough to walk. At seven he was putting in a full day's work at his father's side. He didn't regret his lost childhood because he simply didn't know what he had missed. His father, a sour, hard-working man, had never succeeded at anything and expected no more from life than to scratch a bare living from the unyielding land. His mother was thin, bony, and overworked. There was no time wasted on smiling or the enjoyment of life in the Foxworthy house.

Recalling all these things from childhood brought to him suddenly the knowledge of what the scene in the Stotts' yard had reminded him. The night the Indians came. He and his father and mother had barricaded themselves inside the house, peering out the rifle ports while the Indians deliberately killed the cow and her newborn calf with their arrows, ran down and wrung the necks of the chickens as gleefully as children and beat the head of the sow to a pulp with their tomahawks. Dan's father had not fired at them and it was probably a good thing that he had not. There were close to twenty, and Dan's father's gun was an old Kentucky flintlock that took several minutes of loading and priming between every shot.

Having killed all the livestock, the Indians galloped back and forth across the few acres of half-grown corn until it was completely ruined. Then they burned the smokehouse. They took the smoked meat with them, but they scattered the contents of the root cellar in the yard and trampled potatoes and root vegetables into the ground by deliberately riding their ponies back and forth over them.

Looking back, Dan Foxworthy admitted that his father and mother had deserved that treatment just as much as the Stotts family had deserved to have one of their calves shot down. They had stolen land from the Indians; they had settled it illegally. The Indians had only been telling them to give it back again, to return across the river to where they belonged.

But he hadn't been able to see the Indians' side of it then. He had, furthermore, been less than proud of his father for putting up no resistance as the Indians destroyed everything they had worked so hard to accumulate.

Perhaps it was on that day, at the age of nine, that Dan Foxworthy's intolerance for weakness was born. They stayed on, but because of what they had lost to the Indians, they almost starved that winter. In the spring, other settlers took up land on both sides of them, affording to Dan's family a certain amount of protection and security they hadn't had before. Dan, with youthful intolerance, never quite forgave his father for permitting the Indians to destroy everything they had without so much as raising a finger to stop them.

When he was twelve, Dan ran away from home. His father, needing him, notified the sheriff and two weeks later he was caught and returned. Though his father beat him unmercifully, that same night he ran away again. A second time he was returned and a second time beaten even though the first beating's bruises hadn't healed. He ran away a third time within a week and this time his father let him go. Or else the law just never happened to catch up with him. In any case, he never saw either his father or his mother again. Which bothered him not at all. They had given him no love, and he had given them none. He did not, in fact, know what it was.

He reached the dry bed of Rustler Creek three miles below the Mathias ranchhouse, and followed it in. By the time he reached the place, there was a five-inch covering of snow on the ground.

The barn towered above the other buildings. He dismounted stiffly, brushing snow now from his coat, taking off his hat and batting it against his leg. He led his horse into the barn, removed the saddle and put the animal into a stall. He took off the bridle and hung it up.

A fifteen-year-old boy named Hughie Drumm was working in the barn. Dan said, "Give him some hay and a can of oats. And rub him down."

"Yes, sir," the boy said respectfully.

Foxworthy left the barn and headed for the house. He figured he'd better tell Lutie Mathias what he had done before she heard it from somebody else. He knocked on the back door, then entered without being bidden. He wiped the snow off his boots carefully on the rag rug just inside and removed his hat, which was still dripping. He laid it on the floor beside the door.

Lutie Mathias had been baking bread and the loaves were laid out in two long rows on the table to cool. Their aroma was delicious and suddenly reminded Dan that he hadn't eaten since breakfast. She said, "Take off your coat and sit down. You can have some fresh bread and coffee if you don't think it will spoil your supper."

He shrugged out of his coat and grinned at her. "I don't care if it does. There's nothing I like better than fresh-baked bread."

She was slender and dark-haired, tall for a woman, being nearly five feet ten. Her skin at this time of year was lighter than it usually was, but it still had the golden color given it by exposure to the sun. She had warm brown eyes and a full mouth that seemed made for smiling.

"What was so important that it kept you out this late? I was beginning to wonder if you weren't lost someplace in the storm."

"Lost? Me?" He laughed at the thought, pulled out a chair at the table and sat down. She brought him a cup of steaming coffee and a few moments later a plate of sliced fresh bread and a bowl of fresh-churned butter. He buttered a slice of bread thickly and took a big bite out of it. With his mouth full, he said, "I found another cow."

"Shot?"

"Uh huh. Shot in the neck. That's why I'm late. I rode into town and got Ray Owens and we went back out. Trouble was, the snow blotted out the trail before we reached the end of it." He sipped the scalding coffee, then took another bite of bread. He didn't look at her.

She was studying him, knowing him, knowing there was more. He didn't speak, so at last she said, "You have something more to tell me, haven't you?"

He nodded. "That trail led straight toward the Stotts' place so we kept going even though the trail had petered out."

There now was a wary look on Lutie's face. Dan glanced up at her, a touch of defiance in his eyes. "It's got to stop," he said firmly. "That's over thirty cows we've already found this fall."

"What did you do? You didn't shoot somebody?" There was sudden fear in her voice.

He shook his head, "I killed a calf. I told Floyd Stotts that I'd come there and kill another one every time I found a Pool cow shot."

Her face, now, was pale. "You could have been killed yourself."

He studied her, surprised by the very real concern for him apparent in her face. He was further surprised to see color seeping into her face. She looked away and busied herself at the stove, presenting her back to him.

Belatedly he said, "Ray was there. They wouldn't shoot me with him looking on."

"Ray's not always going to be with you." She turned and met his glance and there was an unexpected vulnerability in her eyes. It startled him and confused him and for once he didn't know what to say. Lutie said, "Every member of the Pool has thousands of cows. It won't hurt them to lose a few. But it *will* hurt them if they lose you."

He heard himself saying, "And you?"

Her glance didn't waver. She murmured, "It would hurt me too."

He stared at her for a long moment, watching the pulse that was visible in her throat, seeing how difficult it was for her to continue meeting his glance. Something was stirring in him that he had never experienced before, something that both confused and puzzled him.

He'd known his share of women, but his relationships with them had always been brief and devoid of sentiment. They gave him something he needed and he paid them for their services. This new feeling was unsettling. He lowered his glance and picked up another slice of bread. He began to butter it, noticing with irritation that his hands were unsteady.

The silence dragged on. He could feel Lutie watching him. Without looking up and keeping his voice as matter-of-fact as he could, he said, "The Pool's range is surrounded by people like the Stotts family. They want it, and they'll get it unless we make them believe they're risking their lives trying to take it away from us."

"What has that got to do with killing a calf?"

He glanced up now defensively. He knew men, and he knew whereof he spoke. "They're probing. If they get

away with killing cows to get their calves, they'll take
to rustling bunches of cattle next."

"What in the world would they do with them? The Pool
brand is known for five hundred miles."

"Over in the mountains they don't pay any attention
to the brand a critter wears. They butcher 'em and throw
the hides down an old mine shaft."

Stubbornly she said, "I still think that you were wrong."

He felt irritation stir in him and said, "There's going
to be a meeting of all the members of the Pool a week
from Saturday. I'm willing to lay it on the line for them.
If you, and they, want me to quit, why then I'll quit."

Her own irritation was audible in her voice. "Nobody
said anything about quitting. I just said I thought that
you were wrong. Do you have to be right in everything?"

He glanced up at her. Her eyes were sparkling. He
grinned and got lazily to his feet. "No. Not in everything.
Just almost everything."

He thought she was going to stamp a foot but she did
not. She said instead, "You are the most exasperating
man I ever met!"

"Yes, ma'am."

"And don't you 'yes ma'am' me!"

"No, ma'am."

Furiously she stared at him. Finally the shadow of a
smile appeared at the corners of her mouth. She said, "Get
out of here. I've got better things to do than argue with
you."

"Yes, ma'am." He went to the door and picked up his
hat. Turning, he realized that he was wishing he could
take her in his arms. He would like to kiss that smiling
mouth. Perhaps she could tell what was in his mind because the smile faded from her mouth. He had the feeling
that if he did go back she would not resist.

Turning, he went out into the snow, closing the door behind him. He tramped across the yard toward the bunkhouse, shrugging into his coat as he went.

He had spent thirty-five years avoiding close relationships. He'd never cared what anybody thought of him. He'd never felt protective toward anyone. He'd never let a need for anyone upset his thinking or his life.

At least not until the last year. Not until he took the job of ramrodding the Cheyenne Pool. He realized now how often, since he came here, Lutie Mathias had been in his thoughts.

An urge as old as time itself was prodding him. He wanted a wife and he wanted a family. Angrily he kicked the snow off his boots and slammed open the bunkhouse door.

CHAPTER 3

Floyd Stotts was a big man, his middle gone to paunch. He never shaved more than twice a week, so he usually had an untidy growth of whiskers on his face. He stood in the snow for several moments after Foxworthy and the sheriff had disappeared, wearing only his red flannel underwear, his pants and a pair of dirty socks through which the big toe of his right foot stuck out.

Floyd was forty-one, the oldest and the acknowledged head of the family. The women were still shrieking, the children crying, the dogs barking, and the men shouting enraged curses in the direction Foxworthy and the sheriff had gone. Floyd was angry too, as much at himself for not having done anything as at Foxworthy for having so arrogantly killed the calf.

He bawled, "Quit the screechin' an' go cut the damn calf's throat! Hang 'im up an' git to butcherin'!"

A couple of his brothers and several of the older boys headed for the body of the calf. Floyd bawled, "The rest of you git back inside! There ain't nothin' more to see!"

They complied a bit sullenly, talking among themselves. Floyd watched, scowling. He wished he'd killed Foxworthy. He'd never get a better chance. There wasn't a jury in the country that wouldn't have called it self-defense. But he hadn't, and now it was too late.

He'd been caught by surprise, just as much as anybody else. He'd snatched up a rifle before rushing out, but he'd been too startled to make use of it. In the first place, he hadn't expected Foxworthy to shoot the calf. He'd been prepared for threats and nothing more. Besides that, after shooting the calf Foxworthy had pointed the rifle straight at him. If he had raised his gun it was likely that he'd now be lying in the snow, as dead as the stolen calf.

While the calf bled, his brothers and the boys helping them went to their respective houses to get their boots and coats. When they came back out, several of them dragged the dead calf into a shed. Floyd turned and headed for his own house, now conscious of his chilled feet. His brother Russ was standing just outside the door. Russ said, "We should of killed the son-of-a-bitch!"

Floyd snarled, "Sure we should! But the bastard pointed his gun at me. He'd a had a bullet in my gut before I got my gun in line! If anybody should of killed him, it should of been one of you!"

Russ stared sullenly at him. Turning away finally, he grumbled, "Sure. Blame it on us."

Floyd ignored him. He went inside, sat down and took off his wet socks. His wife brought him a dry pair and he put them on. He pulled his chair closer to the stove and sat with his feet almost touching it, heels on floor, toes pointing at the ceiling. He was still scowling. Neither his wife nor any of his four children said anything. One of the girls was still sniffling.

Foxworthy's rifle *had* been pointed at him but, he admitted uncomfortably, not all the time. There had been an instant after the Pool foreman shot the calf when it would have been possible to kill him, if he had been ready and if he had not let his fear of the man immobilize him. If he *had* taken a shot at Foxworthy, his brothers would have riddled the Pool foreman before the man could get off any more than a single shot.

More seriously he had, by his inaction, lost face with his family. Russ's voice had held thinly veiled criticism because they hadn't killed Foxworthy. The others were probably feeling equally critical.

He'd lost face, and he'd lose more if he didn't do something to avenge the death of the calf. But what could he do? The Pool was too damned big. They had too much money and too many men. And they had Foxworthy, the son-of-a-bitch!

The fact that the Pool really had no legal right to the land they claimed taunted him. Anyone could legally claim any part of it under the homestead law. And if they claimed the springs they could control the range around those springs for as far as a cow could walk.

The Cheyenne Pool couldn't last indefinitely. Some of the members of the Pool had even admitted it. Well, by God, maybe it was time to break the damn' outfit up. Maybe it was time somebody moved in on them. If everybody moved in at once . . .

Nervously he got up. His feet were warm now, so he pulled on his boots. He got his coat and put it on. He crammed on his hat and went out the door.

It was still snowing, but not as hard as it had been a while ago. He crossed the yard to the shed. The calf was skinned and gutted, hanging steaming from a rafter of the shed. The entrails, which had been allowed to fall on a gunnysack, had been dragged outside for the dogs and cats. Several dogs were picking at them, growling at each other occasionally.

Three of Floyd's four brothers were here, having washed their hands with snow and lighted up their pipes. Russ was one of them. Theron and Sam were the other two. Floyd said, "We've taken all we're going to take from that dirty son-of-a-bitch!"

All three looked questioningly at him. He said, "I think it's time we grabbed ourselves a hunk of their range."

"They'd slaughter us!"

"Not if somebody camped on every one of their goddam springs."

"There ain't enough of us."

"I didn't say just us. I meant everybody. All our neighbors. Everybody that wants a piece."

It was an ambitious plan and nobody knew it any better than did Floyd. But it was a way of regaining face. And it just might work. Particularly if somebody, somewhere, managed to get Foxworthy in his sights.

Russ asked, with the old respect in his voice again, "When do you plan on doin' it?"

"First thing in the morning we'll ride out and talk to everybody we think might be interested. Git 'em to meet in town. We'll talk it over an' then we'll make our plans."

He turned and walked away, calling back, "Be sure an' close them doors before you leave. The dogs'll pull down the calf." He might have regained whatever face he had lost earlier, but he got an empty feeling in his gut when he thought of trying to take range away from the Cheyenne Pool.

He was committed, though, and he didn't dare back out. Angrily he wished that he could have the last half hour to live over again. He'd kill Foxworthy if he did. With Foxworthy dead, it would be easy to seize range from the Cheyenne Pool.

There was half a bottle of whiskey in the house. He got it down and took a drink from it. His wife, bony and overworked, looked at him. "You're plannin' somethin', ain't you, Floyd? You ain't goin' to try killin' him?"

"I will if I git the chance."

"You won't git the chance. He'd kill you first."

"Mebbe not. He's human just like the rest of us."

"If you shoot him in the back, you'll hang."

Turning his head, he snarled, "Who said anythin' about shootin' him in the back? Just shut your mouth, woman. What I do is no business of yours!"

She stared at him a moment and then looked away. Floyd took another drink. He began to think what it would be like to own Indian Springs, six miles north of here on range now held by the Cheyenne Pool. Indian Springs was the only water within a six-mile radius. That meant he'd control a piece of richly grassed range six miles across. About twenty-eight square miles in all. That would support fifteen hundred head of cattle. He wouldn't have to do without any more. He and his family could live like other people did.

His wife lighted the lamps and started supper. Floyd finished the bottle, ate his supper and went to bed. But he couldn't sleep in spite of the whisky he had consumed. He kept thinking about tomorrow. He kept thinking about seizing Indian Springs, scared at the thought, but excited too.

And another thought was growing in his mind. They'd need cattle to stock all that range around Indian Springs. He couldn't use Pool cattle, even if he could steal them from the Pool. But he could take some Pool cattle and drive them to Leadville to the mines. With the money they brought, he could buy cattle with which to stock the newly acquired range. He went to sleep finally, and did not awake until the sky turned gray.

This morning, the clouds were high and gray. It was still snowing fitfully but it was obvious that it was clearing up. Immediately after chores, Floyd's brothers and the older boys scattered, each heading toward one of the neighbors to tell them what was in the wind and to tell them about the meeting that would be held in town. Floyd had set the time for the meeting at eleven o'clock, the place at the Odd Fellows Hall.

Floyd himself rode south to the McKenna place. It was only three miles away, so he reached it before Josh McKenna had left the house.

He told McKenna what was in the wind, watching the man's face turn scared, watching the glint of greed chase the fear from his eyes. Grinning slightly to himself, he turned his horse and headed straight for town.

Arriving, he tied his horse in front of the Red Dog Saloon. It hadn't opened yet, but Pete Valdez was sweeping out. He let Floyd come in and stand at the bar. After a while Tony Schmitz, the owner, arrived. Nervous and jumpy, Floyd ordered a bottle and a glass.

Others began to arrive a little after nine o'clock. At ten-thirty, Ray Owens came into the saloon. He looked at Floyd and then at the half-dozen others lined up at the bar. He asked, "What the hell's going on? What are you all doing here in town?"

Floyd scowled resentfully at him. "Is there some law against it, Sheriff?"

Ray Owens stared back at him. "I don't blame you for being sore about yesterday. I'd have stopped him if I'd known what he was going to do."

"You would like hell! You're just like everybody else in this goddam town! You know which side your bread is buttered on!"

Owens studied him worriedly for a moment. He said, "Don't start anything, Floyd. Foxworthy's tougher than you think."

"He's human. He can be stopped."

Owens grinned humorlessly. "You'd better be pretty

sure of yourself before you try stopping *him*." He turned and went out. The worried look remained in his eyes.

Once outside, he stopped, took out his pipe, packed and lighted it. He puffed thoughtfully for a moment, straining his ears, trying to hear something from inside the saloon that would give him a clue as to what all the Pool's neighbors were doing here. They must have seen his shadow through the window, though, because the place remained as silent as the grave.

He walked up the street. He didn't know what was going on but he knew something was. Every small rancher in the country was in town today. Four of them were up in Holloman's Mercantile. Half a dozen were down in the Red Dog Saloon. Several others, including Floyd's four brothers, were at various places around town. Waiting. For something. For a meeting, probably. And a meeting of the neighbors of the Cheyenne Pool, called by Floyd Stotts today, could only mean trouble. They were probably planning some kind of attack on the Pool.

He went into his office, closed the door, and took off his coat. He shook down the ashes in the stove and added a couple more pieces of wood. He began to pace nervously back and forth.

He hadn't been able to control Foxworthy yesterday. He wouldn't be able to control him any better today. Or tomorrow. Or any other day.

Nor could he control the enemies of the Cheyenne Pool if they acted together and determinedly. He had the sudden, uneasy feeling that an open clash was coming between the two forces. Soon. Maybe as soon as tomorrow or the day after that. And knowing Foxworthy, he was sure the Pool foreman would act as intemperately and recklessly, whatever happened, as he had acted yesterday.

He stopped pacing. He couldn't handle the kind of trouble he foresaw. Not by himself. But he had no help, except for Tom Kirby, who sometimes worked for him as a part-time deputy. The only thing he might do would be to try and head off the trouble before it blew everything sky high. And the only way to do that would be to get the members of the Cheyenne Pool to call Foxworthy off.

With his mind made up, he went out, closing and locking the door behind. He hurried up the street toward the big three-story house at the upper end of town in which Colonel Ireland lived.

Ireland came to the door, dignified and white-haired, and courteously invited the sheriff in. Owens followed him into the parlor and sat down on the edge of a velvet chair. He said, "I think trouble is shaping up, Colonel Ireland. I think you ought to call your Pool meeting early. I think you ought to do it right away."

"What are you talking about?"

Owens told him swiftly about the calf. He told him about all the Pool's neighbors being in town today, adding he was sure it was for a meeting of some kind. He said he figured the only reason for a meeting would be to plan action against the Pool.

Ireland looked worried. "What do you think they'll do?"

Owens said bluntly, "You're holding your land illegally. You and I both know you can't go on doing it forever. I figure whatever they do will have something to do with grabbing off your land."

Ireland nodded. "Thanks for telling me. I'll get word to the other members of the Pool immediately. Perhaps if we compensate Mr. Stotts for the calf he lost . . ."

Owens nodded. "Maybe that'll do it. I doubt it, but it's worth a try."

He headed for the door. Ireland let him out, saying, "Keep me posted, Sheriff, on what's going on."

"Yes sir, Colonel Ireland." Owens put on his hat and headed back down the street.

From here, he could see the Odd Fellows Hall, a block and a half this side of the Red Dog Saloon. He could see the crowd in front, the others crossing the street toward it.

Determinedly he headed toward it. They probably wouldn't let him in, but he was going to try.

CHAPTER 4

When everyone had crowded into the Odd Fellows Hall, Floyd Stotts looked at his brother Russ. "Go guard the door."

Russ walked away. The small ranchers were seated in folding chairs they had taken from a stack just inside the door. Floyd waited until Russ reached the door. Then he raised his hands for quiet.

"Yesterday, Dan Foxworthy an' the sheriff rode out to our place in that damn snowstorm. Foxworthy accused us of killing a Pool cow to get her calf. He hadn't trailed the calf to our place, but he shot one of our calves just the same an' threatened to shoot another every time he found a Pool cow dead."

There was a murmur of talk in the room. Floyd raised his hands again for quiet. He said, "It's about time we stopped taking that kind of crap from the Pool. They got no right to the land they hold. The only one that's got any rights at all is Lutie Mathias, and she's only got rights because her old man filed legally on a one-hundred-and-sixty-acre homestead claim."

A man in the back yelled derisively, "What you goin' to do, Floyd? Take it all away from 'em?"

Floyd fixed his glance on the man. "That, by God, is exactly what we're goin' to do. Unless the rest of you are satisfied with what you got. Maybe *you* don't mind watching their cattle get fat while yours stay thin. But I do. I mind. An' we're goin' to get our share of Pool range whether the rest of you do or not."

The same voice yelled with equal derision, "Yeah? And just how the hell do you think you're goin' to do that? You goin' to ask Foxworthy for it? You goin' to say please?"

Floyd bawled, "Shut your goddam mouth! We got a right to take that range! It's open for homesteading. All we got to do is file on every one of their springs and water holes. We fence the water if we have to. And what do they do when they got no water for their stock?"

"What about the windmills?" another man yelled.

"We file on the land where the windmill is. We can't keep 'em from taking their windmills down if that's what they want to do, but we can keep their cattle from getting any of the water the windmill pumps." He stared out triumphantly at the men in the big room.

From the door, Russ yelled, "Floyd, the sheriff's comin' up the stairs."

Floyd raised his hands for quiet. He called, "Tell 'im he can't come in. Tell 'im this is a private meetin'."

The door opened and the sheriff appeared in it. Russ blocked his way. Floyd could hear him say, "You can't come in. This here's a private meeting."

"Well, I'm coming in."

There was a brief scuffle at the door. Russ was slammed back, staggering, and the sheriff came into the room. He glared at Floyd and said, "What's going on?"

Floyd said, "Like Russ told you, it's a private meeting. You got no right in here. I'm askin' you to leave."

The sheriff stared at him angrily. Floyd said, "We'll do no business while you're here. We can wait just as damn long as you can, Ray."

The sheriff remained where he was for a moment. Then

he shrugged fatalistically. "All right. But I'm warning you. No trouble."

Nobody said anything. Ray Owens turned, walked to the door and went down the stairs. Russ stood looking down until the outside door had closed. Then he turned. "He's gone."

Floyd stared challengingly at the crowd. "Well? How about it? If we all stick together, we can get away with it. They've got Foxworthy and they've got a crew, but they'll be outside the law. Besides that, they can't kick us all off at once!"

Someone shouted, "He can take us one at a time!"

Floyd nodded. "Sure, and that's likely what he'll try to do. So each of you keep someone handy with a horse. When you see him coming, ride for help. Meantime, don't fight him if he kicks you off. Go quietly. Then as soon as he's left, move back on the spring."

"What if he leaves some men there to see that we don't?"

"That's what we want him to do. Time he leaves a couple of men at every spring and water hole, he won't have any left. We can handle a couple of men. We just can't face the whole Pool crew."

Josh McKenna yelled, "Hell, it might work!"

Floyd yelled back, "You're damn right it'll work. Just sing out which of the springs you want, and we'll write 'em down. First thing tomorrow morning, move in on 'em. You'll need four claim stakes, and four pieces of paper to nail to 'em. You'll need a man to stay on the claim, someone to ride to town and file on it, and someone to ride for help in case Foxworthy shows."

The men crowded around the speaker's platform at the front of the hall. Floyd dug out a piece of paper and a pencil stub and began to write their names and the name of the spring they wanted to claim. At the top of the paper he wrote *Indian Springs,* and after it, *Stotts.*

The others began yelling their names and the spring they wanted to file upon. Floyd wrote them down as quickly as he could. There was a lot of pushing and shoving, and for several moments it looked as though fights might break out between some of the men. Eventually, however, the list was made, the takeover decided upon. Floyd stood up and yelled, "All right, go home. Just remember, be on those springs as soon as it gets light. If Foxworthy shows, send someone to my place for help. Don't fight 'em. Let 'em do anything they want. Just remember, we're in the right!"

The men dispersed. As the first of them reached the door, Floyd yelled, "And no damn talking! Understand?"

They filed out and went down the stairs. In five minutes, all that were left were Floyd and his brothers. He said, "All right, now here's what *we're* gonna do. Russ and me are going to help ourselves to a bunch of Pool steers. We'll have 'em in Leadville an' be back with the money before Foxworthy even knows they're gone. That money'll buy us a start in the cattle business."

His brothers were staring at him doubtfully. He said, "Theron, you take my oldest boy, Jess, an' one of yours, an' stake a claim to Indian Springs. Sam, you an' Hal stay home with the rest of the boys, in case anybody sends for help. If they do, send one of the kids for the sheriff. Then you hightail it to wherever the help is needed. If you get the chance, kill that damn Foxworthy no matter how you have to do it."

"How the hell will we git away with that?"

"Kill 'im for a claim jumper. A man's got a right to protect his property, ain't he? After yesterday, no jury in the world would blame us for killin' him. Not if he's tryin' to

take a lawful claim away from us. Or away from any of
the others."

Looking at his brothers, he could see that the face he
had lost yesterday had been regained threefold. Grinning to himself he said, "This calls for a drink. Le's go
down to the saloon."

The five left the Odd Fellows Hall. They walked down
the street to the Red Dog Saloon. Floyd pushed in first,
and his brothers crowded in after him. They went to the
bar. Floyd called loudly, "Give us a bottle, Tony."

Schmitz brought a bottle and five glasses. Floyd poured
one for himself and passed the bottle on. Tony looked at
Floyd curiously. "What's all the people doin' in town
today? Looks like everybody for a hundred miles."

"We had a meetin' up at the Hall."

"What about?"

"What else? That goddam Cheyenne Pool."

"What have they done?"

"What have they done? Yesterday Foxworthy rode
into my yard an' accused me of killin' one of his cows.
Took out his gun an' shot one of our calves. Said he'd do
it again every time he found a Pool cow shot."

"You shoot the cow?"

"Hell no, I didn't shoot the cow. Anybody might've
done it. Plenty of people hate that goddam Pool, that's
sure enough!"

"What did you decide to do?"

"Can't say. But you'll see. The Pool will, too."

Tony shrugged and moved away. Russ, on the end,
leaned as close as he could get and whispered, "How many
cattle you goin' to take?"

Floyd felt big and important. He said, "Three-four hundred head."

Russ whistled. He looked doubtful for a moment, but

as he continued to study Floyd's face, he began to grin. He said softly, his voice hoarse, "You hear that, boys? He says three-four hundred head. That's damn near a hundred head apiece."

Floyd poured a second drink for each of them. Their faces were flushed, their eyes shining. A couple of them kept licking their lips nervously.

They might be nervous and they might be scared, but nothing now could turn them back. In their imaginations they already owned Indian Springs. They had money with which to buy cattle to stock that vast, lush range. One or two of them were already thinking about how they were going to spend their new-found wealth.

Ray Owens sat with his feet on the desk, puffing his pipe comfortably. The pot-bellied stove in the middle of the room gave off a muted roar. Flakes of snow drove along the street horizontally, but the sun was trying to break through, and the snow was thawing on the ground.

Now the wind would blow, he thought, and that might be worse than snow.

He was comfortable and warm, but the frown he wore showed how worried he really was.

What had happened at the Stotts' place yesterday might have seemed like a small thing to Foxworthy, but there had been a lot more to it than the simple killing of a calf. By killing the calf, Foxworthy had challenged Floyd. Worse, he had humiliated him in front of his entire family and Owens knew how strong family pride was among people like the Stottses who had come from the hill country of Tennessee. Floyd would have to regain the face he had lost yesterday. And Owens had the uneasy feeling that the meeting at the Odd Fellows Hall had been concerned with that.

He got up and began to pace uneasily back and forth. Occasionally he went to the window and stared broodingly into the street. Most of the small ranchers had left town immediately after the meeting but a couple of wagonloads of them were still in town, loading up necessities at the store. Floyd and his brothers were down at the Red Dog Saloon.

Owens could see it from where he sat. He could see the horses racked in front, their rumps to the rising wind, tails whipping between their legs. He saw Ossie Robinson come from the saloon and stand for a moment in the wind. Once he glanced back toward the door of the saloon. Then, turning up the collar of his coat and clutching it closed in front of him to compensate for buttons long since gone, he scurried across the street.

Twice he glanced behind, as if nervous or afraid. When he reached the sheriff's office, he looked behind again, before ducking quickly in. He closed the door behind him and stood for a moment with his back to it. He said, "Whew! That wind's mighty cold."

"Sure is. Want a cup of coffee? It's pretty strong, but at least it's hot."

"Don't mind if I do." Ossie was a little man, bowlegged from thirty years of riding, as shrunken as a dried apricot. He had a couple of days' growth of whiskers and he hadn't had a haircut for several months. He crossed the room to the stove, opened his coat flaps in front as if to let in all the heat he could get. He made no move toward the coffeepot.

Owens asked, "What's on your mind?"

Ossie hesitated. He looked at the floor, shuffled his feet and said, "I guess I shouldn't of come."

"Why not?"

"Maybe it wasn't nothing."

"Maybe what wasn't nothing?"

"What I heard."

"What did you hear?"

"I ain't sure I ought to say."

"Was it something about Floyd Stotts?"

"How'd you know?"

"Guessed. What was it, Ossie?"

"They was talkin'. Somethin' about three-four hundred head. They ain't got that many cattle, have they, Ray?"

"Nope. They haven't got more than fifty head in all. What did they say about the three or four hundred head?"

"I couldn't hear too good. I had my head down on a table. I'd been asleep but they woke me up."

"Did they know you heard?" There was immediate concern in the sheriff's voice.

"Huh uh. I didn't raise my head. I waited quite a while before I pretended to wake up."

"What else did they say?"

"One said that was damn near a hundred head apiece."

Owens nodded. Trying to sound unconcerned, he said, "Thanks, Ossie. Thanks for telling me."

Ossie started for the door, but Owens said, "Wait a bit, Ossie. Have that cup of coffee. Don't go out there until Floyd and his brothers leave."

Ossie glanced at him quickly. Owens said, "No harm playing safe. If they saw you coming out of here they might figure you'd heard something."

"What do you think they're goin' to do?" Ossie crossed to the stove, got a tin cup full of coffee and went back to the window.

Owens shrugged. "I don't know, but I'll keep an eye on them." He did know, or thought he did. Floyd had figured out how to regain the face he had lost yesterday. He was going to steal a bunch of Pool cattle, though how he expected to dispose of them, Owens didn't know. Nobody in the plains country would buy a Pool cow without a legitimate bill of sale.

At the mining camps in the mountains, though, they didn't care what they bought. The hides went down a mine shaft someplace and once they were gone nobody could prove who the critter had belonged to previously.

Ossie said, "There they go."

Owens came to the window and stared down the muddy, snowy street. The Stotts brothers untied their horses, mounted, and headed toward home.

Ossie finished his coffee. Owens said, "Thanks again, Ossie." He gave the man half a dollar, which disappeared into the pocket of Ossie's coat.

"Sure." Ossie went out, bracing himself against the wind. Walking swiftly, he returned toward the Red Dog Saloon.

CHAPTER 5

For a while after Ossie left, Ray Owens stood at the window, staring gloomily into the street. The wind had increased and he could hear it howling around the building's eaves. The stove still roared, louder now because of the increasing wind. Snow had begun to blow in the street, accumulating in tiny drifts wherever something broke the sweep of wind.

The sun was still trying to break through, but without much success. "Damn," Owens said to himself sourly, "they would pick a night like this."

He began to pace nervously back and forth. He knew he had to try and prevent the cattle theft. He also had to find out somehow what else was in the wind. The small ranchers hadn't met at the Odd Fellows Hall just to pass the time of day. If he had to guess, and he did, he'd say they intended to try camping on the Pool's springs as a means of seizing range from them.

He wished he had a dozen men. But he did not. He didn't have any full-time deputies. Only Kirby, who worked part time for him whenever there was need. Usually all Kirby had to do was watch the jail when he left town.

Having finally made up his mind, he put on his sheepskin coat, crammed his hat down on his head, and went out into the bitter wind. He strode swiftly up the street and turned the corner. Walking rapidly, he reached Kirby's small frame house shortly afterward, and hammered on the door.

Kirby's wife, plump and smiling, opened it. "Come in, Ray. The coffee's hot."

He went in. "Haven't got time, Mabel. Is Tom around?"

She yelled toward the kitchen, "Tom!" and his voice came back, "I heard. Wait 'til I put on my boots."

Kirby came into the room a few moments later. "What's up?"

"I need you. I think Floyd Stotts is planning to steal some cattle from the Cheyenne Pool. I'm going to try and stop him if I can."

Kirby said, "I'll get my coat." He disappeared into the kitchen again. Mabel Kirby looked at the sheriff worriedly. "It's not dangerous, is it, Ray?"

"I don't think so. We'll try to talk them out of it. They know better than to kick up a fuss."

She nodded, apparently reassured. Kirby came into the room, coat and hat on, buckling his gunbelt around his waist. That done, he got a rifle from the closet and some shells for it off the closet shelf. He dug around until he found a pair of overshoes. He said, "I'll go out back and saddle up my horse. Meet you down at the office in five minutes or so."

Owens nodded. He went toward the front door. Kirby kissed his wife and headed for the back.

Reaching his office, Owens got his own overshoes, a rifle and shells, and a pair of heavy gloves. He removed his hat, tied a scarf over his ears and then replaced the hat. He closed the stove damper, locked the office door and hurried down the street toward the livery barn.

Pete Durfee didn't venture out of the tackroom to help. Owens got his horse and rode him out into the street.

Kirby was waiting in front of the office, back turned to the wind, already looking cold. Owens said, "Let's go."

They rode out of town, taking the road to the Stotts' place. Clear of town, Kirby yelled, "How d'you know they're going to grab cattle from the Pool?"

"Ossie overheard them talking at the saloon."

"Maybe Ossie's wrong. You know how he is."

"I know. I just hope to God he *is* wrong."

Kirby didn't say any more. The two rode in silence, abreast, collars turned up against the biting wind. Snow blew across the road, making wave-like patterns out of the tiny drifts that formed. Owens didn't figure it would be too hard to get Floyd Stotts to call off the cattle theft. All he'd have to do would be to threaten arrest. Or if that didn't work, threaten to tell Dan Foxworthy what was going on.

The sun was a sinking, glowing ball behind the clouds when they arrived at the cluster of shacks on the bluff overlooking Arapaho Creek. No one was visible in the yard. A single dog came out of a shed and began to bark as they rode in.

The door of Floyd's shack opened and his wife stood framed in it, surrounded by three of her children, who peered from behind her skirt. Owens did not dismount. He asked, "Is Floyd at home?"

She shook her head dumbly.

"Know where he is?"

Again she shook her head, but this time there was something new in her eyes, something like the panic of a trapped animal.

Owens said, "If you know, Mrs. Stotts, you'd better tell. I know Floyd is up to something and I think I know what it is. If I find him soon enough, maybe I can talk him out of it."

Still shaking her head, she got out a hoarse, "I don't know where he is."

Owens guessed she was telling the truth. "Anybody else likely to know?"

She gestured toward the nearest of the other shacks. "Ask Theron or Sam."

"How about Russ and Hal? Are they gone too?"

"Russ is with Floyd. Hal is here."

Owens nodded. He rode toward the nearest shack. The door was partway open and he could see Theron Stotts looking out. Theron was a younger version of Floyd, though not as heavy as his older brother was. Owens asked, "You know where Floyd and Russ are?"

Sullenly Theron shook his head.

Owens said, "Might be better for everyone if I find them before they do anything they're goin' to be sorry for."

Theron said harshly, "I don't know where they are. I can't tell you somethin' I don't know."

Owens nodded. He hadn't expected anyone here to tell him where Floyd and Russ had gone. He'd hope to catch them before they left. Now he'd just have to try and guess where they were going, and try to intercept them before they reached the place or before Foxworthy caught up with them.

He turned his horse and rode away, taking the road back toward town. Kirby followed him silently. But as soon as the Stotts' shacks were out of sight, Owens turned north onto range belonging to the Cheyenne Pool. Kirby ranged up alongside. "What now?" he yelled.

"There ain't but one place a man can sell cattle wearin' the brand of the Cheyenne Pool. That's over in the mining camps."

"There's a hell of a lot of mining camps."

"But not too many that can handle three-four hundred head."

"Leadville?"

"I figure."

"Then they'll likely try to drive up Willow Creek to the Arkansas."

"That's the way I figure it."

"And they likely won't reach Willow Creek until tomorrow at the earliest. They got to gather a bunch that's fat enough for butcherin', and they can't drive 'em at night."

Owens nodded. He had turned west, knowing they were far enough north of the Stotts' place so that they would not be seen.

Willow Creek was well west of the range belonging to the Cheyenne Pool. Like most streams in southeastern Colorado, it was dry except when heavy rain or melting snow had flooded it. It had a wide stream bed that seldom carried more than a narrow trickle of water in the middle. On both sides were wide strips of wasteland carved out of the surrounding plain by the river when it was flooding. These were grassy, and contained an abundance of cottonwood trees and brush.

It made an ideal route for driving stolen cattle because they could not be seen readily, because water was available, because grass grew long and thick. There was also shelter from the sweep of wind, both for the drovers and for the cattle themselves.

Owens angled north now, wanting to strike Willow Creek well beyond where Floyd Stotts would enter its bed with his stolen herd. He figured Stotts wouldn't go any farther than he had to go for steers.

Gradually, as they rode, the light faded from the sky. The wind did not decrease. Owens dreaded the coming night. Neither of them had enough blankets. They had no tent, not even a tarpaulin. They didn't dare build a large fire, for fear it might be seen.

Darkness came. The clouds had thinned and a few stars shone through. Owens maintained his heading by using one of the stars as a reference point.

Neither man had spoken for several hours when they finally reached the bed of Willow Creek. Owens said, "Gather up some wood. I'll check to make sure they haven't already gone by."

Kirby dismounted, dropping the reins of his weary horse. He stamped his feet vigorously to restore circulation to them. He flailed his sides and back with his arms, trying to warm them up.

Owens rode on ahead, crossing the grassy bottom, his eyes on the ground. He found nothing, no tracks, no sign that a herd had gone by here. He rode across the sandy stream bed and checked the creek bottom on the other side similarly. He found no trails.

When he returned, Kirby was trying to coax a small blaze to life. He had shaved a piece of dry wood with his knife and lighted the shavings. Now he was carefully adding twigs and larger sticks to the blaze.

Owens squatted miserably across the fire from him. His breath turned to huge clouds of steam. He cursed softly, disgustedly, dreading the coming night, knowing the temperature could dip to around ten degrees.

The blaze grew and began to throw off heat. Owens spread his hands to catch the warmth. When they were warm, he got up, standing so close that the fire made his pants legs steam. He turned himself like a piece of meat on a spit, slowly warming his legs, turned stiff and numb by cold.

Kirby left the fire and went to his horse. He removed his saddlebags and blanket roll. He dug out a coffeepot, a sack of coffee and a chipped, blue enamel cup. Owens took the coffeepot from him and walked to the stream for water. When he got back he found that Kirby had arranged three rocks so that the pot would set on them and heat.

When the water was hot, Kirby added a handful of coffee and the air filled with the aroma of it. Shortly after that, he filled the cup and handed it to Owens, who sipped the scalding stuff gratefully before passing it back again.

Between the fire and the coffee, he began to feel reasonably comfortable. But even though the fire drove the chill out of his arms and legs, nothing seemed able to drive out the chill that lingered in his chest. Something was telling him that tomorrow would not go well.

Angrily he got his blanket roll from behind his saddle and unrolled it at the fireside. He unsaddled his horse and picketed him at the end of his lariat. Kirby followed suit. Both men gathered a couple of armloads of wood to last the coming night. Then, without removing either boots or sheepskins, they laid down and pulled their blankets over them.

Occasionally through the night, one or the other stirred, sitting up only long enough to add firewood to the dying blaze. Owens slept fitfully, dozing, snapping awake, dozing again. The cold feeling in his chest remained, however much he scoffed at it.

He'd been county sheriff for eleven years, during which time he had often been afraid. But never this afraid. He wanted to get up, saddle his horse and take Kirby back to town with him. He wanted at all costs to avoid the coming confrontation with Floyd Stotts and his brother Russ.

But even though he wanted to, he knew that he would not. Enforcing the law was his job, and he wouldn't shirk it any more tomorrow than he had for the past eleven years.

Toward morning, Kirby began to snore. Envying him, Owens remained awake, glad to see the sky turn gray.

He got up then, rebuilt the fire and put another pot of coffee on. When it was brewed, he woke Kirby and then killed the fire so that its smoke would not be seen by Floyd Stotts and Russ. They finished the coffee and Kirby washed and put away the pot. They saddled, mounted, and rode out. An hour later they heard the faint bawling of cattle coming toward them from the south.

CHAPTER 6

As they rode toward the sound, their horses at a walk,
Owens once more felt that crawling uneasiness that had
first troubled him last night. He glanced at Kirby. The
man seemed completely untroubled. Feeling the sheriff's
glance, Kirby turned and grinned. "Lord, it was cold last
night," he said. "I didn't think I'd ever get warm enough
to sleep."

Owens replied sourly, "You did, though. I'm surprised
Floyd didn't hear you snoring and go some other way."

"Was it that bad? Did I keep you awake?"

Owens shook his head. "I wouldn't have slept anyway."

"Why? Is something bothering you?"

Owens hesitated a moment, then shook his head. He
couldn't put it into words. If he did, he'd sound like a
nervous old woman. Floyd wasn't going to give them any
trouble. Faced with discovery, he'd give up the cattle.
He'd turn them over and go on home. He and Kirby could
push the cattle back onto Pool range and then return to
town themselves. There should be no more to it than
that.

The bawling grew louder as they rode. There was a
bend in the course of Willow Creek about a quarter mile
ahead. Instead of cutting across the inside of the bend to
save time, Owens stayed in the middle of the bare and
sandy creek bed. He didn't want to surprise anyone. He

wanted to be plainly seen a long time before he got in rifle range.

He saw the first of the driven cattle when they were about a quarter mile away. The first drover he saw was a boy that looked to be about fifteen, clad in a ragged coat and floppy hat, riding on the herd's left flank. The boy saw them and immediately turned and galloped away out of sight.

Owens pulled his horse to a halt. Kirby looked at him, and Owens could feel the weight of the man's glance. Kirby said, "Something *is* worrying you. Do you think they might kick up a fuss?"

Owens shook his head. "No. I don't think that. But I'm nervous as an old woman. I'm damned if I know why."

"You want me to go on ahead and talk to them? They might be less likely to start something if they knew you were back here out of range."

Owens shook his head. He didn't want to give Floyd the idea they were afraid of him and splitting up would do just that.

The cattle had halted, and now began to spread out in the brushy creek bottom to graze. Owens saw Floyd and Russ galloping toward them. The boy in the ragged coat and floppy hat stayed behind but in plain sight.

Owens unbuttoned his coat and thrust back the flap so that he could get at his gun. Kirby followed suit.

Floyd Stotts and his brother Russ drew their horses to a halt about a dozen yards away. Floyd tried to look surprised. "What are *you* doing out here, Sheriff?"

"I might ask you the same."

Floyd gestured with his head. "You can see what we're doin'. We're drivin' a bunch of cattle."

"Where?"

"Leadville. To the mines."

"Whose cattle?"

Floyd laughed shortly. "Oh, I get it. You think we're stealing them."

"Aren't you?"

"Hell no, we ain't. You think we're crazy?"

"Whose are they, then?"

"They got the Pool brand on them."

"Who gave you the authority to drive them to Leadville?"

"Foxworthy did. I guess he felt ashamed of what happened the other day. Said he wanted to make it up to us. Said he'd pay us each two dollars a day for the time we was gone."

"The Pool don't sell cattle in Leadville."

"They do now. They just got a new contract over there."

"Let's see your bill of sale."

"Bill of sale? Lord, I knew there was somethin' we forgot to get!"

Owens studied Floyd suspiciously. He knew Floyd was lying. What he didn't know was why. The man must know he couldn't get away with a lie. His story could be checked out with Foxworthy and if it turned out he didn't have the authority to drive the cattle to Leadville, he'd be liable to a charge of rustling, with both the sheriff and Kirby as witnesses.

Owens said, "Floyd, I know you're rustling, and you know you've been caught at it. You'll get at least two years in the pen, and so will your brother Russ. You want to tell me what's going on before I haul you in?"

"I told you, damn it. We're working for Foxworthy."

Owens said, "Keep 'em here, Tom. I'll go talk to that kid."

Kirby said, "Sure, Ray."

Owens rode toward the boy. He couldn't understand why Floyd was being so brazen. And not understanding increased his uneasiness. He glanced back once when he was about a hundred yards away. Kirby had not drawn his gun, but it was exposed and he could reach it easily. Floyd's and Russ's coats were still buttoned, making their guns practically inaccessible. But Floyd had a rifle in his saddle boot.

The boy looked white and scared. Owens halted in front of him. "What's your name?"

"Jess."

"You're Floyd's boy, ain't you?"

"Uh huh."

"You want to see your pa go to prison?"

The boy licked his lips. There was panic in his eyes. Owens asked, "Where you taking the cattle?"

"Leadville, sir."

"Why Leadville?"

"Because they ain't fussy about brands up there. They throw the hides down a mine shaft someplace."

"You know these are stolen cattle, don't you, boy?"

"Yes, sir, I know."

Owens nodded. He asked, "Any other men back there?"

"No, sir. Only two of my cousins."

"Go get 'em and head for home."

"What about my pa an' Uncle Russ?"

"Don't worry about them, boy. Just head for home."

"Yes, sir." The boy looked at him doubtfully a moment, then turned his horse and rode back into the brush.

Floyd Stotts watched the sheriff ride away. He knew Owens would get what he wanted out of Jess. He hadn't coached the boy what to say and Jess wasn't clever enough to lie and get away with it.

He glanced at Kirby. The deputy hadn't drawn his gun, but his hand was within three inches of its grips.

He switched his glance to Russ. There was a question in Russ's eyes. Answering it, Floyd shook his head almost imperceptibly.

Kirby stared at the two suspiciously. "What are you two cookin' up?"

"Nothin'. Just waitin' for the sheriff to get back."

"And then what?"

Floyd shrugged. "Jail, I guess, if he means what he says."

His mind was racing. He didn't know how Owens had figured this out, or how he had intercepted them. It didn't matter anyhow. What did matter was that Owens had them dead to rights. He'd caught them red-handed with cattle that did not belong to them. That added up to two years in the penitentiary for both him and Russ, even if the boys got off.

Even worse, it meant Foxworthy had beaten him again, humiliated him again. He was through as head of the family. He might eventually get out of prison and come home, but they'd only tolerate him afterward. They'd never respect him and they'd never listen to what he had to say.

The sheriff was coming back. Floyd knew what he was going to do before Owens got to them. When Owens was close enough, Floyd said, "Well, you got us, looks like. What you goin' to do?"

"You know what usually happens to rustlers."

"It ain't going to help you keep the lid on things if you take us in."

"What do you mean by that?"

"You saw how many was at the meetin' yesterday."

"And?"

"They're all movin' in on the Cheyenne Pool. They're doin' it right now, campin' on springs an' water holes an' filin' claims to 'em."

He saw the quick concern in the sheriff's face. Owens hesitated a moment but finally he said, "All right. We'll forget we saw these cattle. You two take your three boys and get the hell out of here. Kirby and me will see that the cattle get driven back where they belong."

Russ looked intensely relieved. He headed his horse back toward the cattle. Owens and Kirby followed him, for an instant presenting their backs to Floyd.

It was the chance Floyd had been waiting for. Stealthily, he withdrew his rifle from the boot. He levered a cartridge in.

Owens and Kirby both heard the sound. They whirled in their saddles, awkwardly snatching for their guns as they did. Floyd raised the rifle and sighted it.

He saw the panic touch Kirby's eyes. He saw a kind of fatalism in the sheriff's, as though he had somehow expected this. He fired the instant his sights centered themselves on the sheriff's chest.

The bullet drove a gust of air from the sheriff's lungs. His body jerked violently from the force of the slug, and he dropped his gun and grabbed for the saddle horn with both hands.

His horse, startled by the sound of the shot, shied, nearly unseating him. Then he galloped away.

But Floyd wasn't looking at the sheriff any more. He was sighting on Kirby's chest even as the deputy's gun came up. He fired an instant before Kirby did and once more saw the violent effect of the heavy slug, which smashed through Kirby's breastbone and then went on to sever his spine before exiting.

Kirby was dead before he could grab the saddle horn.

He slid from the saddle as the horse shied, and hit the ground like a sack of grain.

Floyd's horse was already in motion as he did. Floyd raked him with the spurs, forcing him into a hard run across the sandy stream bed, through the brush and cottonwoods that lined it, and up out of the bottom to the level, grassy plain. He caught the sheriff's horse before he had gone three hundred yards, and hauled him to a halt. The sheriff, still alive, still clinging with both hands to the saddle horn, stared at him with pain-wracked, accusing eyes. He didn't say anything. He only licked his lips a couple of times as though he intended to try. But no words came out.

Blood had leaked through the sheriff's underwear and shirt and had spread to make a stain the size of a big man's hand. Floyd turned his horse and rode back, trailing the sheriff's horse behind.

He heard a choking sound just as his horse started down into the creek bottom. He turned. Owens had released the saddle horn. He was trying desperately to extricate his rifle from the boot. As his horse went down the steep incline, he lost his balance and fell forward onto the horse's neck, then sliding to one side as the horse smelled blood and shied with sudden fear.

He struck the ground, weak and unable to speak, but still alive. Floyd released the sheriff's horse and sat his own mount looking down, waiting for Owens to die. Owens moved his lips, trying to speak, but no sound came out. It was plain even to Floyd that had he been able to speak, it would not have been to ask for mercy or for help. He would have cursed his killer with his dying breath.

The eyes of the two locked and held. Floyd realized with some surprise that this was no worse than killing a cow. And he'd thought killing a man would be difficult.

He heard Russ coming and turned his head. Russ was staring at Owens with blank horror, seeming to be in a kind of daze. His voice came out hoarse and cracked, "For Christ's sake, what have you done?"

Floyd snarled angrily, "I've kept us out of jail, that's what!"

"He was goin' to let us go!"

"Sure, if we'd give the cattle back. Well, I ain't goin' to give 'em back, and I ain't goin' to jail!"

Russ started to dismount. "He's still alive. We got to help . . ."

Floyd shouted, "Let 'im alone! Let the son-of-a-bitch die!"

"Then what you goin' to do? How you goin' to cover up a thing like this?"

"Just turn their horses loose with the saddles on an' reins draggin'. It's sure to snow again before they get back to town. People will think Owens and Kirby had an accident. They won't be found 'til spring. If they ever are."

"How you goin' to bury 'em? We ain't got shovels an' the ground's froze hard."

"I'll figure somethin' out. Go back an' put a rope on Kirby an' drag him over here."

Russ stared at him unbelievingly for a moment. He avoided looking at Owens again, and so did not see that Owens finally had died.

Floyd looked around for someplace they could hide the bodies. About a hundred yards upstream, there was a place where a dry wash ran into the creek bottom from the plain. On the north side of the wash, where the sun hit it, the ground would be thawed, he thought. They could pull dirt down over the bodies with their hands.

Not until the floods came next summer would the dirt be washed away and the bodies again exposed. By then there'd be no proving who had been responsible.

He dismounted and put the loop of his rope around Owens's body beneath the arms. Mounting, he dallied the rope and dragged Owens toward the wash's mouth.

He saw Russ coming, dragging Kirby's body similarly. He saw the three boys looking on from a couple of hundred yards away, their terror apparent in the way they stood.

Fleetingly he wondered what his son Jess would think of him. Firmly he put the thought out of his mind. It was time Jess faced some of the realities of life. This was one of them.

CHAPTER 7

Since the horses would not go into the narrow wash, Floyd and Russ had to dismount. Floyd dragged the sheriff's body in first. He went in about fifty feet before he let go of him.

The sheriff's eyes were still open. Dirt had gotten into them and muddy dirt was encrusted on his face. His mouth had come open, and dirt had also gotten into it. Floyd rolled him over against the north wall of the wash, thinking what a damn waste it was to bury the sheriff's wallet with the man. He didn't go through Owens's pockets, however, because he knew what Russ would say.

He went back. Russ looked as though he was going to be sick. He had been half-heartedly trying to get the rope off Kirby but he hadn't been able to. Kirby's eyes were open. Blood had drenched his chest, and still welled out of the cavernous wound in his back. Floyd threw off the loop and got hold of Kirby's wrists. He dragged the man into the wash and piled him on top of Owens, close against the wall of the wash so that a minimum of earth would be required to cover them.

Behind him, he could hear Russ vomiting, gagging, and retching until he almost felt sick himself.

Standing on the bodies, he began to claw dirt down from the bank above them. He had been right in his estimate. It wasn't frozen; it was only damp. It came down easily, and in a few minutes, both bodies were covered.

But he didn't stop. He didn't think either wolves or coyotes would bother the bodies, but it was possible. He wanted to cover them well, so that the smell wouldn't attract anything. He didn't want a bunch of buzzards circling overhead if it could be helped.

He worked hard and steadily for almost half an hour. By the time he had finished, his hands were raw and he was drenched with sweat. But the bodies were covered with at least a foot and a half of well-packed earth.

He sat down on the mound for a moment to catch his breath. It had been easy getting rid of the sheriff and his deputy. It ought to be as easy getting rid of Foxworthy. All he had to do was wait for an opportunity and be ready when it came.

He got up and returned to Russ and the horses. Russ's face was shiny with sweat. He looked at Floyd as if he was afraid of him. Floyd said, "Come on, let's go. We got four hundred cattle to get to Leadville."

Russ mounted and followed him toward where the herd was grazing placidly. The three boys looked at Floyd the same way Russ had, as if they were afraid of him. He said angrily, "What the hell you all lookin' at me that way for? All I done was what had to be done. We had a choice, either give up the cattle or go to jail."

Russ said weakly, "We could of given up the cattle and got some more later on."

"Sure. With Owens watchin' us, an' Foxworthy knowin' what we tried to do."

Russ said, weakly for all the determination in his eyes, "It was murder, Floyd. Neither one of them even had a chance."

"Two against one is murder? Was either of them shot in the back?"

"They barely had time to turn around."

Floyd stared at him disgustedly. "Ah, shut up. What's done is done. You can go back if you don't want a share in what these cattle bring."

Russ stared at the ground sullenly. He said no more, and he did not offer to go back. They bunched the herd and once more pushed them north down the course of Willow Creek. The horses that had belonged to Ray Owens and Tom Kirby cropped grass unconcernedly in the creek bottom for a while. Then, occasionally cropping a mouthful of grass as they went, they headed toward town. The reins of both horses were dragging and they were forced to travel with their heads held to one side so that they would not step on them. The sounds of cattle bawling gradually faded out in the distance, leaving on this vast and empty plain only the sound of the wind sighing through the knee-high grass.

Joshua Ireland had left the Army of the Confederacy with the brevet rank of colonel, but unlike many of his compatriots, he had not left the defeated Confederacy with only his horse and the clothes upon his back. A year before the surrender of Lee's Army at Appomattox Courthouse, he had foreseen the inevitable and had converted the holdings of his family, not into Confederate currency but into gold and gems, which he had managed to smuggle west in his wife's capacious carpetbag, a little on each of her numerous trips to visit non-existent relatives. There was nothing dishonest about it. He was simply being smart.

He was able, therefore, to set himself up in the cattle business in Texas immediately after the war. But, since he didn't like living under Union Army Bluebelly rule, he converted everything he had into cattle and trailed them north toward Abilene.

Only he hadn't gone to Abilene. He went to the south-eastern part of Colorado Territory where there were endless miles of grass that nobody had so far claimed. He had released his cattle on the land now claimed by the Cheyenne Pool. Only one other rancher was there at the time, Lutie Mathias's father, who now was dead.

Ireland had prospered. He had a big house in town, two carriages, a high-stepping team of bays and a fine sorrel Kentucky stallion for riding purposes. He had stocks and bonds and a substantial amount of money in the bank. He had been glad to help form the Cheyenne Pool and turn his cattle over to it. Doing so had relieved him of the necessity of worrying about them himself. Furthermore the arrangement had been very profitable. He had banked more money since the formation of the Pool than he ever had before.

He was practical enough, however, to know that it couldn't last. They didn't own the land on which their cattle ran. Eventually settlers would file homestead claims on it and that would be the end of the Cheyenne Pool. He just wanted to delay the end as long as possible.

He drove himself out to Lutie Mathias's house to tell Foxworthy that the sheriff had suggested they have their meeting right away. The bays stepped out briskly and, with his thick buffalo coat, the colonel was comfortable except that his face got chilled.

Foxworthy came from the bunkhouse in shirtsleeves and stood beside the colonel's rig while the colonel said, "There was a big meeting in town this morning. The sheriff thinks the small ranchers are getting ready to grab our land. He thinks we ought to have our meeting right away."

"You mean today?"

Ireland shook his head. "Tomorrow will be soon enough."

"I'll tell Lutie. What time?"

"Nine o'clock?"

"We'll be there."

Lutie Mathias came to the back door and called across the yard, "Won't you come in, Colonel Ireland?"

"No thank you, Lutie," he boomed. "If I want to get back to town before dark, I'd better move along."

She waved at him as he drove out of the yard. Foxworthy crossed to the kitchen door and went inside. He sat down straddling a chair, his arms resting on its back. "Ireland wants to have the Pool meeting at nine o'clock tomorrow. I told him we'd be there."

"Is something wrong?"

"Owens thinks the small ranchers may be getting ready to grab off our range."

"And what do you think?"

"I think he might be right."

She studied him a moment, plainly liking him but as plainly exasperated. "The calf yesterday?"

He grinned. "That would be the simple explanation, wouldn't it?"

"You don't think it's the right one?"

He shook his head. "It may have precipitated things, but you and I both know this was inevitable. The Pool doesn't own that land. I've tried to get the members to file on it, but they always put it off."

"What can we do? If the small ranchers decide to file on it?"

"Stop them," he said shortly. "We hold it. We use it and claim it. The Pool members ought to have the first chance to file on it."

"What if the small ranchers beat the Pool members to it? What if they file first?"

He said, "I think you know the answer to that."

"You'd rip up their stakes?"

"I'd do anything I had to do."

"Including shooting anyone who resists?"

He studied her face. She was pale and her mouth was firm. Her glance held his determinedly. He said, slowly and carefully, "If I'm shot at, I'll shoot back. I won't shoot first."

"What if the Pool members don't want to fight?"

"Then they can tell me so. I'll quit."

"Quit because they won't do what you want them to?"

He shook his head. "No. It's their show. I'd quit because there wouldn't be any more Cheyenne Pool."

"What would you do?"

"I've always had a job. I'm not worried about myself." He studied her so closely that her face turned pink. She tried to hold his glance and failed. She looked away.

He said, "You're fighting me. Why?"

She raised her glance. "Maybe I don't agree with the things you do."

He grinned faintly. "Still harping on that calf?"

"I'm not harping and I'll thank you not to say I am."

Grinning still, he murmured, "Sorry."

Her eyes flashed. "Don't be so damned superior! You could have been wrong about that calf. You don't know for sure that it was driven to the Stotts place. You didn't trail it there. And if you were mistaken, I wouldn't blame Floyd Stotts for being mad."

"Neither would I. Only I wasn't wrong."

Once more, he thought she was going to stamp a foot. She was angrier than he had ever seen her. She stood there trembling for several moments, fighting for self-control. He found himself wanting her more than ever. Angry like this, she was magnificent. He said softly, "You're a beautiful woman, Lutie Mathias."

For an instant she stared unbelievingly at him. Then a smile touched the corners of her mouth. An instant later she was laughing uproariously.

He crossed the kitchen to her and put his arms around her, forgetting for the first time the invisible line that separated them. She was warm, and soft, and she raised her head, surprise tempering her mirth.

He kissed her, startled at her immediate response. Her arms went around his neck, tightening, but after a moment she removed them and pushed against his chest. He drew away, stirred and wanting more. Out of breath and shaken, Lutie said, "No, Dan. No."

He released her. He wanted to pursue this, but something told him this was not the time. It had happened suddenly, with no warning, and whatever their feelings were toward each other, time was needed for each to sort them out. Lutie wasn't a saloon woman who, just because he had stirred her, would go to bed with him. And he didn't want her that way anyhow. He wanted Lutie permanently, for always. He wanted her for his wife.

He nodded. "All right."

"You're not angry?"

"No. I'm not angry."

"I'll be ready in the morning."

He nodded, and turned toward the door. With his hand on the knob, he swung around and looked at her. And suddenly, unexpectedly, he grinned.

"What does that mean?" she asked.

"Mean? Does it have to mean something?"

Her own eyes twinkled. "Knowing you, I'd say it does."

"Then you puzzle over it." He opened the door and

stepped out into the icy wind. Walking rapidly, he crossed the yard toward the bunkhouse.

The chances were good, he thought, that the Pool members would just fold up and quit. If they did, he was out of a job.

But if most of them elected to go on . . . then he was in for one hell of a fight. He opened the bunkhouse door and stepped inside, wondering if Lutie would support him or if she would not. At the moment he wouldn't have bet a dollar either way.

CHAPTER 8

Dan Foxworthy and Lutie Mathias drove into the town of Wootenburg a little before nine. The sky was clear this morning. The sun was shining, but it gave off little warmth. The wind still blew, drifting snow across the road, sending it swirling into the streets from accumulations on the roofs of the houses and buildings inside the town.

Foxworthy halted the buggy in front of the Wootenburg Hotel. He got down and helped Lutie to alight. Then he clipped a tether weight to the horse's bridle and followed her inside.

Colonel Ireland was in the lobby. He greeted Lutie warmly and directed them to one of the private dining rooms where the meeting was to be held.

Most of the other Pool members were already present in the room. Lutie was the only woman. The air was blue with cigar smoke for which several of the men apologized.

Ireland waited until a quarter past nine. Then he closed the doors and faced the others. "I was hoping Ray Owens would be here but it doesn't look as if he will."

Virgil Whitaker asked, "What is this all about? Why was the meeting called so suddenly?"

Ireland said, "Ray talked to me yesterday. It was he who suggested that we meet today. He said that Floyd Stotts and the other small ranchers who do not belong to the Pool had a meeting yesterday down at the Odd Fellows Hall. Ray seemed to think they were planning to seize our range."

"Seize our range? How in the world . . . ?"

Foxworthy got to his feet. "You'd just as well hear all of it. A couple of days ago, I found another Pool cow shot. Whoever shot her dragged her calf away. I came into town and got Ray and we followed the trail, but the snow blotted it out." His voice now took on a faintly defensive tone. "The trail was headed straight for the Stotts place so we went there. I shot one of their calves and served notice on them that I'd kill another for every Pool cow that we found shot."

Colonel Ireland interrupted: "Ray thought that perhaps if we compensated Floyd Stotts for the calf, he'd call off whatever plans he had . . ."

It was Foxworthy's turn to interrupt. "He would like hell! He'd take that as a sign of weakness, and he'd be exactly right!"

Now everybody began to talk at once. Ireland let them argue back and forth for a few minutes before he raised his hands. "Does anybody want to say anything?"

Foxworthy said, "I do."

Ireland said, "All right, go ahead."

Foxworthy said, "Owens thinks they're going to try grabbing off our range and he may be right. But it's not because of a single calf, and you know it's not. We don't own that range. Except for Lutie, none of you has any legal claim to it. I've urged you to file homestead claims on the springs and water holes, but you put it off. Now it may be too late. If they move in on all our water holes and make it stick, we're finished."

John Masters, burly and grizzled and thick as the trunk of an ancient pine, rumbled philosophically, "We've always known this time would come."

Meyer Garth said, "It's been a good thing while it lasted but we've known the life of the Pool was limited. None of us is poor. It isn't the end of the world."

Foxworthy's anger stirred. He said, "Damn it, you'd better not give up so easily! If they take your water holes you're not even going to have a chance to liquidate in an orderly way. You'll have to drive the cattle to Denver and dump them on the market for whatever price they'll bring. And at this time of year it won't be much!"

Whitaker said, "He's right. We'd have to take half what the cattle are really worth."

Ireland nodded. "I have not always approved of the things Dan has done, but he's been a good foreman and he is right. We have to try holding on until next summer at least. Otherwise we will lose too much!"

Once more there was a babble of talking in the room. Ireland let it go on until it died out by itself. Then he said, "Anybody else want to say anything?"

Nobody spoke so the colonel said, "Then we'll take a vote."

Foxworthy said, "Before you do, there's something else you ought to think about. You've got nearly fifty men working for the Pool. They won't be able to find jobs in the middle of winter. They've been loyal to the Pool and it seems to me the Pool ought to return that loyalty."

Nobody said anything. A few looked guilty and Dan knew these few would vote to liquidate. Ireland asked, "Ready for the vote?"

Several voices indicated that they were. Ireland said, "All in favor of holding on, even if it means a fight, raise your hands."

A scattering of hands went up. Foxworthy counted them hastily, relieved to see that Lutie's was one of them.

Ireland said, "Opposed?"

Other hands went up. Foxworthy swiftly counted them. There were two fewer than there had been before. Ireland said, "Looks like we hold on." He glanced at Dan. "It's up to you. You're the Pool foreman and we'll back you in anything you do."

Foxworthy nodded. He knew he could rely on the colonel's word. He knew the Pool would back him, that even those who had been opposed to holding on would abide by the decision of the majority.

Some of the Pool members went into the hotel bar. Foxworthy and Lutie went out and climbed into the buggy for the drive back home. Foxworthy knew they had no time to lose. He had a hunch the small ranchers were already moving onto the various springs and water holes.

Driving out of town, he took a different road. Lutie glanced at him questioningly, and he said, "Indian Springs. I just want to see if they've moved in yet."

He kept the buggy horse at a brisk trot for more than an hour. The wind seemed to have picked up velocity. Lutie sat with her collar turned up around her ears, her face red with cold.

The road, only two narrow tracks, wound across the open prairie. It was close to noon when they reached Indian Springs. Foxworthy halted the buggy on a rise and stared down at it.

Indian Springs lay in a natural bowl, half a mile across, in the center of which were two small ponds. There were two wagons down there beside the ponds. Stakes had been driven at the four corners of the homestead claim, visible because of the papers tacked to them, fluttering wildly in the wind. A pile of lumber had been unloaded from the wagons. A square had been laid out on the ground close to the ponds, undoubtedly the foundation of a shack they meant to build.

At this distance, Foxworthy couldn't tell who the squatters were. He clucked to the buggy horse and started down the slope.

Lutie asked worriedly, "What are you going to do?"

"Run them off. What else?"

"There are three of them."

He stopped the buggy. "You get out and wait."

There was exasperation in her voice. "That's not what I meant. You can't go up against three men with guns. They'll get behind those wagons and kill you as you ride in."

"What would you suggest?"

"Let's go back to town. We'll find the sheriff and bring *him* out here."

"How do you know he'll back us?"

"He always has. It's worth a try. Please, Dan."

He stared at the figures down below, then turned his head and looked at her. Finally he shrugged. "All right. But if Ray won't help, I'll do it my way. Do you agree to that?"

Reluctantly she nodded. He turned the buggy and headed back toward town.

They had been seen, he knew, but it was doubtful if they had been recognized. He didn't suppose it would hurt to give the law a chance. But if Owens refused to support the Pool's claim to Indian Springs, then he'd feel free to take care of it himself.

They rode in silence for a long time. At last Lutie asked, "Are you angry, Dan?"

He turned his head. "No. I'm not angry."

She smiled and hugged his arm companionably.

Foxworthy didn't question whether he had the right to file on Indian Springs. He didn't question whether he had the right to drive the Stotts family away so that he could. Ownership of land was vested in whoever claimed and held it until the law or the courts decided otherwise. The Stotts family might have squatted on Indian Springs, but he doubted if they had yet registered their claim with the land office in town. The first thing he must do, then, was to make such registration impossible. Even before he brought the sheriff into it. Before he did another single thing.

He held the buggy horse to a steady trot all the way to town. Arriving, he took Lutie immediately to the hotel. "Get yourself something to eat. I'll talk to Ray and then I'll come on up."

"You won't leave town without seeing me?"

"No."

He helped her down and watched her hurry into the hotel. Then he climbed into the buggy, turned around and headed down the street toward the land office. It was nearly two o'clock and he knew it was possible that the Stotts family had already filed their claim to Indian Springs.

The land office, a tiny room, was warm from a glowing pot-bellied stove in the middle of the room. Lance McFee, the land agent, looked up from his desk, a green eyeshade over his eyes. "Hello, Dan. What can I do for you?"

"Any homestead claims been filed today?"

McFee looked surprised. "No. Why?"

Dan felt enormously relieved. He said, "I hear the duck hunting is mighty good down along Willow Creek."

McFee looked puzzled. Dan said, "I want you to go hunting, Lance. I want you to stay gone for at least a week."

"What are you talking about?"

Foxworthy said, "I'll lay it on the line. There's a land grab going on."

"For the range held by the Pool?"

Foxworthy nodded.

"Then I can't leave now. I have to be here to record claims. The Pool has no legal right to that land, Dan. Anybody can file on it. I'm surprised nobody has so far."

"They haven't because I won't let them. And I won't let them now."

"You can't stop them."

"Can't I? Who appointed you, McFee?"

McFee's face lost color. His eyes began to look like those of a trapped animal. Dan said, "The members of the Pool are mighty influential men. Cross them, and somebody else will be sitting in that chair. You think on it."

He turned his back and walked to the window. He stared out into the bleak, windswept street. He watched a woman hurry across, coat whipping in the wind, a shawl clutched tightly over her head. He said, "They're backing me, McFee. Every member of the Pool is backing me. They took a vote."

He stared into the street for several moments more. He knew his time was running out. At any minute, somebody might arrive to file a homestead claim. But he acted as though he had all day. Finally he turned. "Well?"

McFee nodded miserably. "All right. I'll go hunting. I'll stay gone for at least a week."

"Tell me where you'll be in case I want you. The members of the Pool might want to file some claims."

"I'll be on Willow Creek. That old soddy about twelve miles west of here."

Dan saw a wagon coming into town. He recognized the

driver as Hal Stotts. He said, "Get going, then. Out the back door. Give me your key and I'll lock up."

McFee glanced out the window and saw the wagon too. He snatched his coat and hat from the tree, flung his eyeshade on the desk and scurried for the back door. Dan followed and locked it after he had gone out.

He returned to the front of the store. He sat down at the agent's desk.

The wagon pulled to a halt out front. Hal Stotts got down and came inside. He stared at Dan, startled and surprised. "Where's McFee?"

"He was called out of town. Won't be back for at least a week."

Hal started to say something, but as Dan stood up, he seemed to choke on the words. He mumbled something, turned, and went back out the door. He climbed to the wagon seat, turned around in the street and headed back in the direction he had come.

Dan followed him out. He turned, locked the door and pocketed the key. He climbed into the buggy and drove toward the sheriff's office. He'd prevented Hal Stotts from filing on Indian Springs. But they were still camped out there and as long as they were, they had a valid claim.

CHAPTER 9

The door of the sheriff's office was locked. Foxworthy stood for a moment on the walk, hesitating, wondering where the man might be. Then he climbed back into the buggy and headed for the Red Dog Saloon.

Leaving the buggy, he went inside. A quick glance around the room revealed that Ray Owens wasn't here. Foxworthy crossed to the bar. Tony Schmitz was tending it and Foxworthy said, "Whiskey."

Tony brought a bottle and glass. Foxworthy asked, "You seen Ray Owens?"

"Not lately. Why?"

"Need him. Got any idea where he might be?"

Schmitz shook his head. Foxworthy poured himself a drink. Schmitz returned to the other end of the bar.

Sensing someone beside him, Foxworthy turned his head. Ossie Robinson had sidled up and was now looking at the bottle hopefully. Foxworthy said, "Get your glass, Ossie, and pour yourself a drink."

"Thanks, Mr. Foxworthy. Don't mind if I do." The dried-up little man hurried to the table where he had been sitting and got his glass. He brought it to the bar and poured it full. Foxworthy asked, "Seen anything of Ray Owens today?"

"Not today, but I seen him yesterday."

"Where?"

"At his office."

"What were you doing at his office?"

"Went there to tell him somethin'."

"What?"

"You won't say?"

"I won't tell anybody."

"I went there to tell him what I heard them Stotts brothers talkin' about."

"What was that?"

"I heard one of 'em say, 'three-four hundred head.' Then I heard another one say that was damn' near a hundred head apiece."

"What did the sheriff say?"

"Thanked me."

"That was all?"

"Yes, sir, that was all."

Foxworthy finished his drink and put a quarter on the bar. He said, "Thanks, Ossie," and went out the door. Based on the conversation Ossie had overheard it sounded as if the Stotts brothers were planning to do some rustling. It must have sounded that way to the sheriff too. He had probably ridden out to the Stotts place to put a stop to it. If he had, he would undoubtedly have taken Tom Kirby along with him.

Dan drove the buggy to Kirby's house, got down and clipped the tether weight to the horse's bridle. Kirby's wife Mabel answered his knock and invited him inside. He declined. "No time, Mabel. Tom around?"

She shook her head. "He went with the sheriff yesterday."

"Where? Do you know?"

"I don't know where they went. Out to the Stotts place, I suppose. Ray said he'd heard something about Floyd Stotts planning to steal some cattle from the Pool. But

I'm getting a little worried about them, Dan. They were gone all night."

"I wouldn't worry. If they're hunting Floyd it would take at least that long."

"Will you look for them?"

"I can't, Mabel. I've got too many other things to do. Squatters are on Indian Springs and they're probably on every other spring as well. But Ray and Tom likely are all right. They probably just had to stay out overnight."

"I suppose you're right." But the worry did not leave her eyes.

Foxworthy looked down at her for a moment. Finally he said, "Tell you what. If they're not back tomorrow, I'll send some men to look for them."

Her face turned warm with gratitude. "Thank you, Dan. That relieves my mind."

Foxworthy went back to the buggy, unclipped the tether weight and returned it to the buggy floor. He climbed in, clucked to the horse and headed for the hotel.

Ossie had said, "three-four hundred head." With that many, there was only one place Floyd could go. There was only one place that would be able to handle that many with no questions asked. Leadville.

Owens must have figured it out the same way. He also must have guessed that Floyd would probably drive to the Arkansas by way of Willow Creek, thence up the Arkansas to Leadville. Owens and Kirby had probably ridden ahead, planning to intercept Floyd somewhere on Willow Creek.

His guesswork could, of course, be wrong. He'd find out tomorrow. In the meantime he had troubles of his own. He tied the buggy in front of the hotel and went inside.

Lutie was sitting in the lobby, reading a newspaper. She glanced up. "Find him?"

Dan shook his head. "He got wind of some rustling by Floyd Stotts and he and Kirby left town."

"When?"

"Yesterday."

"And they're not back yet?" Lutie's expression was worried.

"They couldn't be. If Floyd and his brothers took as big a bunch as I think they did, they'd have to take 'em to Leadville. The best way is down Willow Creek to the Arkansas. Ray would have figured that out. He'd probably get ahead of them and wait."

"Then you think he's all right?"

"I don't know why he wouldn't be." But inside he wasn't as sure as he sounded. Floyd Stotts was mean and unpredictable. Faced with prison for rustling, there was no telling what he might do.

Lutie said, "Maybe we ought to telegraph Denver for a U.S. marshal."

Foxworthy shook his head. "If we do, we're sunk. He'd back the squatters because they're already on the land."

"Then what are you going to do?"

"Nothing today."

"And tomorrow?"

He said, "Lutie, you know what has to be done. They've got to be moved off those springs. Soon as they are, we'll file our own homestead claims. We can file 'em in the names of the hands. We'll worry later about who eventually gets title to them."

"What if they file on the claims before you can drive them off?"

He grinned down at her. "They won't."

"Why?" Her expression was wary.

"Because Lance McFee just went duck hunting for a week. By the time he gets back, we'll be in possession of the springs again."

There were mixed feelings in her glance, as if she admired his resourcefulness while deploring his ruthlessness. Foxworthy said, "Let's go home."

She nodded and got to her feet. He followed her out, and helped her up to the buggy seat. Climbing up himself, he slapped the horse's back with the reins.

They rode in silence for a long time. At last, Lutie said, "I'm worried about Ray."

"Ray can take care of himself."

"Are you sure? Floyd Stotts is mean."

"Floyd's a thief, but he isn't dangerous. He hasn't got the guts to be dangerous."

"I wish I could be as sure as you."

"If Ray isn't back tomorrow, I'll send some men out to look for him."

She nodded, apparently satisfied with that. Hunched against the cold, they drove on, arriving at the Mathias ranch in early dusk. Foxworthy helped Lutie out at the back door of the house. He drove to the barn and told Hughie Drumm to unhitch the horse and put him in his stall. Then he went to the bunkhouse.

It was almost as big as the barn. The first room was a huge dining hall, with tables and benches enough to seat nearly a hundred men. Beyond this, on the left, a door led to the kitchen, where food for the hands was prepared. On the right, a hallway led to the crew's sleeping quarters. Here there were forty or fifty two-tiered bunks, about half of which had mattresses and blankets on them.

A door, opening off the hallway between dining room and sleeping quarters led to the office of the Cheyenne

Pool, where the records were kept, where the huge iron safe was, where Foxworthy had his desk.

He also had a bookkeeper, a thin, bespectacled man named Bob Hiller. Hiller was hunched over a desk writing, wearing a green eyeshade to shield his eyes from the glare of the lamp.

Hiller glanced up as Foxworthy came in. "Hello, Dan."

Dan nodded. He hung up his hat and coat, crossed the room and backed up to the stove. On top of it a coffeepot simmered. Warmed, he got a cup and poured it full.

He said, "I need some men to file homestead claims for the Pool. You go through the names you've got and come up with about twelve that we can trust to turn them back to us."

"All right." Hiller studied him briefly. "They finally decided they'd better file, huh? Or did you decide?"

"Stotts and his friends decided for us. Stotts is on Indian Springs. I have an idea the others have squatters on them too."

"What are you going to do?"

"Run 'em off."

"What if they've already filed?"

Dan grinned. "They haven't. McFee's left town."

A faint smile appeared on Hiller's mouth. "At your urging, I suppose?"

"It wasn't his own idea." He gulped the last of his coffee and went back into the dining hall. There were about twenty men sitting around, drinking coffee, talking, some playing cards. Dan said, "I need all the men I can get tomorrow to drive squatters off the springs. How many are down at the old Ireland place?"

A man spoke up. "Must be a dozen or more."

"Ride down there after supper and tell 'em to come back here. How about the Brunner place?"

"Eight or nine." It was the voice of another man. Dan said, "You go fetch them. Swing by the Masters place on your way back. Get anybody who's there."

The men at the three places and those here would give him more than forty men. It ought to be enough.

He sat on the end of a table and idly watched the progress of a poker game. But he couldn't keep his mind on it. He was worried about the sheriff and his deputy.

Why the hell hadn't Owens come to him for help, he wondered. But his wondering was short-lived because he knew the answer. Owens didn't trust him not to fly off the handle the way he had at the Stotts place the other night. Rather than risk a killing, Owens had gone himself, taking only Tom Kirby, his deputy.

Uneasily, Foxworthy admitted that if anything had happened to Owens, it would be, partly at least, his fault. Owens was doing the Pool's dirty work. He ought to be getting help from the Pool.

He got up and walked to the window. Gloomily he stared outside. He could see the square of light in the darkness made by the kitchen window at the house.

If he drove the squatters off the springs and had a few trustworthy hands file on them, he could extend the life of the Pool by a good many years. But he couldn't extend it indefinitely. Sooner or later the pressure for land would become too great. Deeper wells would be dug and windmills erected and their strangle hold on the springs would no longer be enough.

He should begin to think of his own future, he realized. Unless he wanted to go back to drifting from job to job.

He thought of Lutie again and stared at the square of light across the yard. He saw her pass between the window and the light.

He wondered if a marriage with Lutie could succeed.

She didn't always approve of the things he did. And he wasn't sure he could change.

The cook and the cook's helper came in and began to set the tables. Dan went to his accustomed place and sat down to wait. He had a feeling, not a reassuring one, that the next few days were going to settle a lot of things, including what his future relationship with Lutie Mathias was going to be.

CHAPTER 10

At dawn, the yard at the Mathias ranch was busier than it had been for months. Horse wranglers ran a herd of seventy or eighty horses into the huge round corral. Men crowded the gate, holding bridles or hackamores in one hand, ropes in the other, waiting their turn to catch a mount from the wildly galloping bunch inside the corral. Having done so, they led them out, saddled and mounted, riding out the bucking that almost always preceded the day's work.

By the time the sun was up, Foxworthy had assigned groups to the various springs and given them instructions as to what they were to do. The instructions were simple. Ride in, destroy stakes and evidences of settlement, drive out the squatters by whatever means were necessary. He stressed that trouble was to be avoided if possible. But the springs were to be reclaimed, whatever the cost might be.

He himself selected three men to go with him to Indian Springs. One was a bow-legged Irishman named Hannigan. The second was Red Elder. The third was a burly, silent, and sometimes sullen man named Dutch Franz. Dan was riding out leading the three, when he heard Lutie call to him from the house. He said, "Go on. I'll catch up," and rode back to see what she wanted.

Standing on the back stoop in the raw November wind, she stared at him silently, plainly having changed her mind about what she intended to say to him. He waited patiently until at last she said, "You'll be careful, won't you, Dan?"

He grinned. "That wasn't what you called me here to say."

"No. It wasn't. I was going to ask you not to . . ." She stopped, then said, "It sounds awful when I put it into words."

"You were going to ask me not to hurt anybody if it could be helped."

She nodded.

He said, "I won't. The truth is, I can't blame those people for trying to take land away from us. It's just my job to see that they don't get away with it."

"Be careful of yourself, too."

He nodded. "Everything will be all right."

She gave him a faint smile and he turned his horse and rode away. He looked back from a couple of hundred yards and could see her still standing there, her skirts whipping in the wind.

He caught up with Hannigan, Dutch, and Red about a half mile from the house. They were maintaining a steady trot. Hannigan glanced at him and asked, "Think they'll fight?"

Foxworthy shook his head. Floyd, smarting under what had happened the other day, might have put up a fight. But Floyd wouldn't be present at Indian Springs. Floyd was on his way to Leadville with two or three hundred Pool steers. Unless Ray Owens and Tom Kirby had already intercepted him. Unless they had turned him back.

He urged his horse to a gallop and the three with him kept pace. Even so, it was past nine when they crested a low rise and looked down into the wide, shallow bowl that contained Indian Springs.

He had eased up the rise so that only their heads would be visible from below, unnoticeable to those camped on the springs. He stared down now, marking in his mind the three stakes that were visible from here, their notices fluttering in the wind. There were two wagons at the springs, the same wagons that had been here yesterday, but this morning the Stottses had erected the framework of a shack and were busy nailing clapboard on. They gave no sign of having seen Foxworthy and those with him.

Foxworthy turned his head. "Let's go. Keep your guns ready, but don't shoot unless they shoot at you."

The three nodded to indicate they understood. Foxworthy dug spurs into his horse's sides and thundered down the slope.

They had gone nearly a hundred yards before those down below heard them and glanced up. Immediately they dropped their tools. They grabbed their guns and scurried into the partially completed shack.

Hannigan pulled in close beside Foxworthy and yelled, "I ain't so sure I like this. They got cover an' we ain't. They could slaughter us."

"They won't! They know better than to shoot!"

Hannigan pulled away, his expression saying he was not so sure. Foxworthy let his own horse forge out in front. They were close now, close enough to see the barrels of rifles sticking out of the unfinished door and window openings in the walls of the shack.

Foxworthy flipped back the skirt of his sheepskin and drew his gun. He thumbed the hammer back as his horse came to a plunging halt before the shack. He said harshly, "Come on out, but shuck your guns before you do!"

There was an instant of silence. One of the guns in the shack was trained on Foxworthy's chest. He could see a scared young face behind it, and he held his horse very still, half afraid to breathe. He waited as long as he dared and then repeated, "Shuck your guns and come out. Nobody's going to get hurt as long as nobody shoots."

Once more the silence dragged, but the rifle muzzle that had been trained on Foxworthy's chest lowered slowly and he breathed a long, slow sigh of relief. The gun dropped to the dirt floor inside the shack and a trembling boy of about thirteen came out, his hands held well away from his body.

Foxworthy risked a glance at the men with him. All were holding their guns, all with their hammers back, but none looked nervous enough to shoot. Foxworthy said, "Come on, the rest of you. Come out and drop your guns."

Hal Stotts came out, emptyhanded, followed by his brother Sam. Foxworthy asked, "Where's the rest of them?"

"Theron went to town."

"How about Floyd and Russ?"

Hal shrugged, but his eyes would not meet Dan's. "Home, I guess."

"You guess wrong. They're on their way to Leadville with a bunch of Pool steers."

Hal's glance raised. His eyes met Dan's and for an instant showed him the fear in them. Then Hal looked down again. Foxworthy asked, "Anybody else inside that shack?"

Hal turned his head. "Come on out, boys."

Two more boys came out. One appeared to be no more than ten. The other was about fifteen. Both had shotguns, and both stooped and laid them on the ground just outside the door.

Foxworthy said, "Get your horses and get going."

The horses, four of them, still with the harness on, were tied to the wagon wheels. Hal and Sam untied them and drove them into position ahead of the wagons preparatory to backing them into position. Foxworthy said, "No. Just mount up and ride out."

Hal looked up at him sullenly. "What are you goin' to do?"

"Never mind. Mount up."

"You wouldn't shoot if I said no. You wouldn't shoot an unarmed man."

Foxworthy shoved his gun into its holster. He took down his rope. "No. I wouldn't shoot an unarmed man." He shook out a loop.

Hal stood his ground sullenly. Foxworthy tossed the loop. It settled over Hal's head and Foxworthy instantly yanked it tight and dallied it, reining his horse away quickly enough so that Hal was prevented from throwing off the loop. Hal hit the ground sliding, yelling, "All right! All right! We'll go!"

Foxworthy halted his horse. He let Hal get up and throw off the loop. The three boys had already mounted, the two younger ones on one horse, the fifteen-year-old on a second. Hal mounted one of those remaining, Sam the other one. Foxworthy said, "Get going."

They rode away, heading south. Hannigan asked, "What about this junk?"

"Burn it. It ought to cost them something to try taking land away from us."

The three men dismounted. One lifted the first of the wagon tongues. The others got on either side. They pushed the wagon up close beside the shack. They went back for the second one and pushed it against another wall.

Foxworthy glanced at the four work horses and their riders, now halfway up the slope. He could see the white faces of Hal and Sam and the three boys looking back. He hesitated only briefly before he said, "Gather up the lumber that's left and the scraps. I don't want anything left."

They picked up the lumber that remained, piece by piece and threw it into the shack. When they had finished, Foxworthy dismounted. Fishing a match from his pocket he went into the shack.

There were scraps and pieces enough to kindle a small fire against the wall. He did so, then stood back and watched while it grew in size. He went outside, once more glancing up the slope.

The Stottses had halted their horses and were watching the thin plume of smoke that curled from the doorway, to be whipped away on the cold November wind.

Foxworthy's mind was no longer on the wagons and the shack. He was thinking about the sheriff again, and worrying.

He mounted and rode to the first of the stakes the Stottses had put out. Dismounting, he scratched out Floyd's name and wrote his own. He mounted and rode to the second stake and after that the third and fourth. When all the notices had been changed, he rode back toward the now furiously blazing shack.

A thick column of smoke was rising from the wagons and the shack. The wind whipped it away and rolled it over the rim of the shallow bowl that contained Indian Springs. The flames crackled with a series of noises like pistol shots. Glancing south, Foxworthy saw that the Stottses had disappeared.

Hannigan, Dutch, and Red were standing a hundred feet away from the shack but even at this distance the heat was noticeable. Foxworthy said, "Dutch, you and

Red stay here until you're relieved. Hannigan, come with me."

Dutch asked, "What do we do if they try to take it back?"

"Don't let 'em."

Dutch nodded. Hannigan mounted and followed Foxworthy up the slope toward the southern edge of the small, natural bowl. Before he went over the rim, Foxworthy glanced behind.

The roof of the shack collapsed, sending a shower of embers high into the air. Dutch and Red had unsaddled their horses and were leading them to the spring. A bunch of cattle came over the far rim of the bowl in single file, heading for the water and a drink. They stopped and stared at the men and at the blazing pile of embers, which was all that now remained of the two wagons and the shack. Then, more slowly, they came on.

Foxworthy turned his face toward town, promising himself that if Ray Owens wasn't there, he'd put finding him ahead of everything else.

CHAPTER 11

It was close to noon when Foxworthy and Hannigan rode into Wootenburg. The train was just pulling out, its whistle a mournful sound carried on the wind.

Snow still lay unmelted on the north sides of houses and buildings and where the drifts had been unusually deep. The street itself was a sea of mud which had been frozen last night but which now had thawed.

Foxworthy went to the sheriff's office first. It was still locked and showed no sign of life. Immediately, he turned his horse and rode down the street to the Red Dog Saloon.

Hannigan was grinning with anticipation as they went inside. Foxworthy led the way to the bar, unbuttoning his sheepskin as he did. Tony Schmitz looked questioningly at him and he said, "Whiskey. Two glasses."

Tony brought them. Before he had even poured a drink, Foxworthy asked, "Seen Ray today?"

Schmitz shook his head.

Foxworthy dumped some whiskey into Hannigan's glass and some into his own. He asked, "Know anyone that has?"

Again Schmitz shook his head. "You think somethin' might've happened to him?"

"No. I need him is all."

"Hell, he's gone lots of times for several days."

Foxworthy nodded. He didn't want to stir people up

unnecessarily but he was now very worried. He put a hand on Hannigan's shoulder. "Stay here. Wait for me, but don't get drunk."

"Sure, boss." Hannigan was grinning. Foxworthy put a dollar on the bar. "Drinks are on me. Just remember, don't get drunk. I might need you later on."

Hannigan was already pouring himself another drink. Foxworthy went out into the everlasting wind. He untied his horse and mounted, then headed straight for Kirby's house. He rode up the alley, dismounted and went to the back door. Mabel Kirby answered his knock.

Her face was unusually pale and her eyes were red from weeping. Foxworthy asked, "Is Tom still gone?"

She nodded wordlessly, tears filling her eyes. She tried to speak, swallowed, then finally managed to say, "Dan, I'm scared. I'm so scared that something has happened to him."

Foxworthy tried to sound more reassuring than he felt, "I doubt that, Mabel. But I'll send some men out to look."

Her face showed her relief.

Dan said, "Don't worry. I'll try and let you know something yet tonight."

Her gratitude embarrassed him. He returned to his horse, mounted and headed back down to the center of town. He'd get Hannigan, he thought, and then round up some of the men who worked for the Pool. He suddenly remembered how scattered they were. It would take all the rest of the day just to round up enough men to mount a search.

Two horses were standing in front of the sheriff's office and he felt a quick surge of relief. One he recognized immediately as Ray Owens's horse. The other was probably Kirby's. Both men must then be safe.

He urged his horse to a fast trot. When he was still half

a block away, he saw that neither horse was tied. The broken ends of their reins dangled and the saddles of both were covered with mud.

He dismounted, and approached them, speaking soothingly, his rope in his hand. He slipped the loop around the neck of the sheriff's horse, then turned his attention to the saddle.

Covered with mud it was, but Foxworthy wasn't looking for mud. He examined it carefully for a moment, occasionally rubbing away a bit of dried mud. What he found was blood, just a little of it, smeared on the saddle horn.

He turned and went to the other horse. On this saddle he found no blood, even though he looked for it carefully.

Returning to his own horse, leading the sheriff's, he mounted and rode to the Red Dog Saloon. Kirby's horse followed the sheriff's like a dog. Foxworthy dismounted at the saloon, tied his horse and the sheriff's and went inside.

Hannigan had made good progress on the bottle. It was a third empty. Foxworthy felt a mild irritation but he didn't say anything about the amount Hannigan had consumed. Instead he said, "Go down and ring the fire bell. Tell everybody that Ray Owens's and Tom Kirby's horses have come back riderless. Tell 'em there's blood on the sheriff's saddle and that I'm taking out a posse to look for him."

Hannigan, his face alarmed, turned and hurried from the saloon. Schmitz, who had overheard, asked, "Anything I can do?"

"Yeah. Ask any of these men who are sober enough to get horses, rifles, blankets, and some grub. Meet back here in half an hour."

He hurried from the saloon. He untied his horse and

returned to Mabel Kirby's house, leading her husband's horse by one of the broken reins. He hated what he had to do, but he knew when she heard the fire bell it would terrify her more than anything he could say.

She must have been looking out the back door because she came hurrying across the yard. Foxworthy dismounted and led Kirby's horse toward the small stable behind the house. Her voice barely audible, Mabel asked, "Tom? Is he . . . ?"

"I don't know, Mabel. His horse and the sheriff's just came in. From the looks of them, they've been traveling quite a while."

"Is there . . . was there . . ." Her terrified glance clung to the saddle on Tom Kirby's horse.

Foxworthy said, "There was a little blood on the sheriff's saddle, Mabel, but none on Tom's. I looked it over good."

She nodded. She was trembling violently from head to foot. He said, "Get back inside. I'll put Tom's horse away."

He led Kirby's horse into the stable. He threw the saddle over a stall partition and hung the bridle up. He gave the horse some hay, then went out into the yard and pumped a bucket full of water. He carried the bucket back and dumped it into the horse's trough. He closed the door and headed for the house.

Mabel was sitting at the table in a straight-backed chair. Her head was buried in her arms and she was sobbing. The fire bell had begun to ring urgently, but she didn't raise her head.

Foxworthy put a hesitant hand on her shoulder. He said, "Mabel, don't give up. Tom is probably all right."

She raised her head. There was a hopeless expression in her eyes. She said, "Tom is dead."

Foxworthy didn't know what to say to her. He went out, closing the kitchen door. He went next door to the neighbor's house and knocked. Mrs. Matson, a widow, answered his knock and Foxworthy said, "The sheriff's and Tom Kirby's horses came in riderless. Mabel's sure that Tom is dead. She needs somebody to be with her."

Mrs. Matson was already reaching for a shawl. She came out and hurried toward the Kirbys' back door.

Foxworthy mounted and rode back toward the main part of town. The fire bell had stopped clanging. There was a crowd in front of the Red Dog Saloon. About a dozen of the men already had horses and were ready to go. Some were examining the sheriff's saddle. Without dismounting, Foxworthy asked, "Would one of you take Ray's horse down to the livery barn?"

A man untied the sheriff's horse. Holding one of the broken reins, he handed Foxworthy's rope up to him. Foxworthy looked carefully at the men who had assembled here. Hannigan was a little unsteady, but he'd sober up as they rode. The rest looked competent. He knew most of them, some of them pretty well. He asked, "Have you all got plenty of blankets and grub?"

They all replied that they had. Foxworthy asked, "Anybody see these horses come into town?"

A man called out that his wife had seen them wandering down the street.

"Which way did they come from?"

"North."

"Let's go, then. Let's see if we can pick up their trail." He knew that backtracking the two horses was going to be a long, drawn-out process, with no guarantee of success. Judging from the way their saddles looked they had rolled in the mud more than once. Their reins were broken and frayed. They might have been wandering for a couple of days and nights.

But if he wanted to find Ray Owens and Tom Kirby in time, he had better follow the horses' trail. Owens and Kirby might be hurt. They might need help desperately.

He led out of town, carefully watching both sides of the road. It was muddy and pocked with the tracks of horses. But luck was with him. He had gone no more than a hundred yards when he spotted two sets of tracks entering the road from the west.

Following them, it was almost immediately evident that these tracks were those of the two loose horses that had just wandered into town. They were aimless. They zigzagged back and forth and sometimes Foxworthy found a place where the horses had stopped, or where one of them had cropped a mouthful of dried grass not covered by drifts of snow.

He kicked his horse into a lope. In the muddy earth, the trail was plain and easily followed, even at a gallop. And while the two loose horses had wandered erratically, their general direction had always been southeast, toward the town of Wootenburg, which was home to them.

Behind him, more than a dozen men swept along, grim and serious, each suspecting what Foxworthy did, that Owens and Kirby were either badly hurt or dead.

The afternoon slipped away. Foxworthy and his posse passed well north of the Stotts ranch, crossed the corner of land claimed by the Cheyenne Pool, and left it finally ten miles short of Willow Creek.

At the crown of a bluff, Foxworthy halted his horse to rest and the men strung out behind caught up and halted too. Hannigan, looking a little sick, said, "It's beginning to get dark."

"Yeah. I don't suppose we've got more'n an hour left."

"What are you goin' to do?"

Foxworthy looked at him, feeling helpless, angry because he did. He said, "Nothing much we *can* do but camp. We can't trail these horses in the dark and we don't dare give up the trail."

"What do you suppose he an' Kirby were doin' 'way over here?"

"Owens heard that Floyd Stotts was planning to steal three or four hundred head of beef. He figured they'd go to Leadville with 'em, that being the only place that would touch 'em without a bill of sale. Best way to Leadville is down Willow Creek and up the Arkansas."

"And you think Owens and Kirby caught up with them? That they've been shot?"

"That's my guess."

"But you think they could still be alive?"

Foxworthy shook his head. "I don't think so, but it's possible."

"Why the hell would Floyd turn their horses loose?"

"Probably figured there'd be a snow before they got back to town. Figured they'd never be trailed back here."

Hannigan glanced at the gray cloud bank that had built up to the west. "Before morning, we could have that snow."

Foxworthy knew that if the trail was lost, the bodies of Owens and Kirby might not be found until spring, if they were ever found. He kicked his horse into a gallop again, slid him down the slope off the bluff, and streaked across the plain below, still following the trail. As he rode, he cursed helplessly to himself. He wasn't going to make it to Willow Creek tonight. And if it snowed . . .

Worriedly he watched the gray clouds ahead, trying to decide which way they were moving. They seemed to be drifting slowly south, spreading eastward as they did.

He tried to make himself relax. He couldn't control the weather, and they couldn't travel any faster than they already were. Whatever happened was in the hands of fate. He and the others could only do their best.

But he promised himself one thing. Whether he found the sheriff and Kirby or not, he was going on toward Leadville after he had conducted a thorough search. He could overtake the stolen cattle, because they could travel no more than fifteen or twenty miles a day.

And when he did, he was going to call Floyd Stotts and whoever else was with him to account.

CHAPTER 12

Foxworthy gave up the trail and spurred his horse hard for the last five miles, knowing the animal could rest when they reached Willow Creek. He particularly wanted to arrive before dark because he wanted to see what trails were there.

Dusk lay deep and heavy across the snowy landscape when he finally put his weary horse down the cutbank into the bed of Willow Creek, his eyes studying its floor even as he did. He rode fifty yards before he came to the first of the cattle trails. They were unmistakable. Farther on, he found the tracks of two horses overlying those the cattle had left.

His men straggled down into the creek bed. Foxworthy dismounted and said, "We'll make camp. Tomorrow we'll look for trails."

He unsaddled his horse, watered him and picketed him where there was grass. By now it was completely dark. Some of the men had busied themselves gathering wood and building fires. Foxworthy carried his saddle to one of the fires and laid it down.

They would find the trail of the two wandering horses again in the morning, he thought. They would be able to backtrack them to the place where Owens and Kirby had been killed. No longer did he doubt that the sheriff and his deputy were dead. The trail of the stolen cattle had driven all lingering doubt from his mind. All that remained now was to find the bodies and establish the cause of death. After that, he'd take some of the men and go after the rustlers.

Hannigan asked, "You want us to take torches and look for tracks?"

Foxworthy shook his head. "We'll have to stay here overnight anyway. The men are beat and so are the horses. I figure Owens and Kirby have been dead at least three days. Another night won't hurt."

"You do think they're dead, then?"

"Can't see much hope they're not. Several hundred cattle were driven past here and the trail of the sheriff's and Kirby's horses came from here. I can't add it up any other way."

"What are you going to do when you catch up with them?"

Foxworthy hesitated. His direct-action tactics in killing the calf had precipitated this, in part at least. Direct action against the rustlers might very well precipitate more violence. He said, "Take them back to town. Put them in jail."

Hannigan stared at him. "I thought maybe you'd hang the bastards from the nearest tree."

Foxworthy smiled faintly. "A week ago that's probably what I'd have done."

"What changed?"

"I figure killing Floyd's calf is what set him off. I guess maybe I pushed the man too far. I made him look bad in front of his whole family and he had to do something to make himself look good again."

Hannigan was studying him closely. "That kind of talk don't sound like you."

"Maybe it's time I changed." He turned and walked away, liking neither the way Hannigan was probing him, nor the way Hannigan's probing had set him to examining himself.

He'd spent his whole life, he thought, pushing as hard as he had in order to get what he wanted out of life. But how many times had his pushing precipitated violence on the part of those he pushed? How many times, like now, had others suffered for something he had begun?

He paced furiously through the darkness. Finally he began to gather wood and, loaded with all he could carry, went back to the fire where his saddle was.

Most of the men had already turned in. Hannigan lay with his back to the fire, snoring softly. Foxworthy added some wood sparingly, then got his own blanket roll from behind his saddle. He laid down and pulled the blanket over him. He closed his eyes, but he didn't go to sleep.

Parading in his memory was the scene the night the Indians came to the farm in eastern Kansas where his father and mother had settled earlier. And the scene in the yard at the Stotts place on Arapaho Creek the night he killed the calf.

One lousy calf, he thought. One small retaliation for a much larger wrong. Yet because of it, Owens and Kirby were probably dead and their killer would hang for his crime.

Lying there staring up into the cold night sky, Foxworthy realized with a shock how empty his life had been. He had lived only for the work he did, only for himself. He had made no close friends. He had made no close attachments with women. He had no children.

Sourly he thought that all he had was the Cheyenne Pool. Well to hell with it. Things were going to change. He was going to change.

Change. He chuckled softly to himself in the darkness. How does a man change the pattern of years when he is thirty-five? Well, first of all, he'd ask Lutie Mathias to marry him. He could learn to be less intemperate. He could learn to consider someone else besides himself.

For the first time he thought about Lutie in terms of what she thought and what she felt. She must have been desperately saddened by her father's death. She must have been very lonely since his death. But until now he hadn't thought of that.

He went to sleep finally, but it was an uneasy sleep because he was very cold. Occasionally he wakened and fed the dying fire with sticks he had laid nearby. When dawn came, he was up, moving around, standing over the rebuilt fire trying to get warm.

The men made coffee and cooked the food they had brought with them. Foxworthy drank two cups of coffee and ate some of the bread one of the men gave to him. Then he mounted and rode out, heading back alone in the direction from which they had come, trying to pick up once more the trail the loose horses had made.

He picked it up half a mile short of the place they had abandoned it last night and at a gallop followed it back to the bed of Willow Creek. The possemen intercepted him and he ordered them to fan out in a circle and search. He himself stayed with the trail of the two loose horses and shortly afterward came upon the muddled jumble of tracks made by the rustlers. Boot tracks and the smudged trail of something being dragged led to the mouth of a dry wash that fed into the bed of Willow Creek. Knowing what he was going to find and dreading it, Foxworthy drew his gun and fired three rapid shots into the air.

The possemen came galloping. Hannigan dismounted and Foxworthy said, "Come with me."

He walked into the wash, following the boot tracks and

what now appeared to be two separate, smudged trails. He found the mound beneath which Floyd Stotts had buried the two men. He stopped and stared down at it, feeling sick at his stomach and lightheaded. He turned his head and yelled, "Two or three of you come in here. If you've got anything to dig with, bring it along."

Several of the men came crowding curiously into the wash. Foxworthy pointed to the mound. "Dig 'em up. That's where they are."

There was icy, controlled rage in his voice, but it was not wholly rage at the murderers. It was anger at himself as well. Floyd's loss of face with his family over the shooting of the calf had triggered the rustling. And the rustling had resulted in the deaths of the sheriff and his deputy.

Nobody had anything with which to dig, but the earth was soft. They dug with their hands, and as they did, Foxworthy turned his back and stared back down the wash at the rest of the posse, clustered so curiously forty or fifty feet away.

He was not surprised when a man called from behind, "I hit somethin'," and a moment later, "It's a boot. There's a spur on it."

The fury now was building to a crescendo in Foxworthy. And an impatience was building along with it. He wanted Floyd and he wanted Russ. He wanted to put them on horses and stand the horses underneath a cottonwood and hang them there and leave them so that all the country could see what happened to rustlers and to murderers.

From behind he heard the man's voice again, "It's Kirby, Dan! Owens must be the one underneath!"

Foxworthy didn't say anything. He couldn't. His throat seemed to be shut off. How the hell was he going to tell

Kirby's wife that he was dead? How was he going to tell her· that her husband had been murdered and buried like a dog? He knew what both Kirby and Owens would look like when they were carried out of the wash. Their clothes would be covered with loose, damp earth. Their eyes and noses and mouths and ears would be filled with it. So would their hair. He realized that he was shivering as if he was very cold.

He heard movement behind him and stood to one side while three men carefully carried out the body of Tom Kirby. Foxworthy didn't want to look but he forced himself.

He'd seen dead men before, so it wasn't a new experience. Even so, the sight hit him like a blow.

Earth was, indeed, all over Kirby's clothes, clinging to them. But it also filled his eyes, and nose and mouth. None of the men had been able to force themselves to clean it away.

Foxworthy followed them out of the wash. They laid Kirby gently on the ground. Knowing this was something he had to do, Foxworthy knelt and gently brushed the damp earth out of Kirby's eyes, off the rest of his face. Only when he had finished, did he stand up. The men of the posse were looking at him strangely, as if they could not believe what they had seen.

Back in the wash, another voice yelled, "The other one's Owens, Dan. Shall we bring him out?"

"Bring him out!"

They came out carrying the sheriff and laid him beside Kirby. Foxworthy said, "We ought to have a wagon, but it'll take too long. Load 'em onto horses and take them back to town. Some of you will have to ride double going back."

A man asked, "What are you going to do?"

"I'm going after the rustlers. I want half a dozen men, but if any of you have got ideas about lynching anybody, don't bother to come along."

The same man yelled, "The sons-of-bitches don't deserve a trial! They didn't give the sheriff and Kirby a trial, did they?"

"They're going to get one anyway."

One of the men led a horse over to where the bodies lay. The horse snorted and tried to pull away. While one man held him, two others lifted Kirby's body preparatory to loading it on the horse. Having been in the ground, it was not frozen, but rigor mortis had set in and the body was stiff as a board. The men laid it down again. "This ain't going to work, Dan. We'll have to get a wagon no matter how long it takes."

"Lance McFee is in that soddy five or six miles south of here. He'd have a buckboard I think."

"What the hell's McFee doing there?"

"Duck hunting. Tell him to stay there. I'll send the buckboard back to him."

A man rode away, heading south at a steady lope. Foxworthy looked around at the shocked faces of the men. "Who wants to go with me?"

Hannigan was the first to reply. "I'll go." Half a dozen other men spoke up. Several were silent, shocked by the violence that had occurred and wanting no more of it. Foxworthy said, "There will be no lynching. Is that understood?"

The response was grumbling, but they all agreed. He said, "And no shooting that isn't necessary. I want them both alive."

Again he got the grumbling assent. He said, "All right, then. Let's go."

Leading them, he rode north at a steady trot, following

the bed of Willow Creek and the plain trail of the four hundred rustled steers. The trail was at least three days old, but that didn't worry him. Four hundred cattle weren't going to cover much more than ten or twelve miles a day. He and the six men who rode with him could cover sixty if they didn't have to follow trail.

They ought to catch up with the stolen cattle by dark tonight, or early tomorrow at the latest.

CHAPTER 13

Foxworthy held his horse to a steady trot, staying on the dry sand of the stream bed because it made easier going for the horse. The men, seven in all, followed him in a ragged group, some calling back and forth, some talking quietly among themselves as they rode. There was no excitement in them, only a grim purposefulness. Not a one but had known both Owens and Kirby. Not a one but had liked both men.

The hours dragged. Occasionally Foxworthy let his horse walk, but always he urged him on to a trot again. In midmorning, they found where the rustlers had camped three nights ago. Shortly after noon they found where they had camped night before last. In late afternoon, they found the place where the rustlers had camped last night.

Plainly, the rustlers were driving harder than before. Foxworthy could imagine them hurrying along, looking back sometimes to see if they were being pursued.

He halted at five, unsaddled his horse and rubbed him down and instructed his men to follow suit. Afterward, he picketed the animal to graze and laid down to sleep. Hannigan growled, "What the hell are we stoppin' for? We can catch 'em in an hour or two if we try."

"What for? They're not going to get away."

"How do you know that?"

"They don't know anybody's following them."

"It's stupid to wait. I say let's get 'em an' get it over with."

"You'll do what you're told. Or you'll go back."

Another man asked, "Why *are* you stoppin', Dan?"

"To rest. Us and the horses both. Some of you can build fires. We haven't eaten since morning and we likely won't get another chance until tomorrow."

"You going to hit 'em in the dark?"

Foxworthy shook his head. "I'd like to locate them while it's dark but if we hit 'em then there's too much chance they'll get away. We'll surround their camp and wait for first light when they're just rolling out of bed."

He closed his eyes wearily. He thought of Ray Owens, remembering the day he'd gone in to town and forced Ray to ride out to look at the dead cow with him. He thought of Ray and Tom being hauled to town in the back of Lance McFee's buckboard. He thought what it was going to be like for Mabel.

He dozed, and awoke, and got up. Hannigan poured him a tin cup of coffee and he sipped it appreciatively. Hannigan had some meat cooking in a pan. When it was done, he shared it with Foxworthy.

The sun went down behind the distant, snowy peaks of the Continental Divide. Hannigan and the others cleaned their dishes with sand and repacked them behind their saddles. They looked at Foxworthy expectantly.

He said, "Wait. Wait until it's dark. I want us to see them before they see us."

Light faded slowly from the sky. At last, when it was fully dark, Foxworthy got up, coiled the picket rope and saddled his horse. He mounted and waited until the others were ready. Then he said, "No talking. We'll hold it to a walk, and we'll ride on the sand so we won't make any noise."

He led out, the men shadowy behind him, visible as darker blotches against the whiteness of the sand. There was only the soft hissing of hoofs in sand and occasionally the clink of metal as one of the horses shook his head.

Head sunk on chest, Foxworthy rode broodingly. Had he been wrong all along? Those who belonged to the Cheyenne Pool didn't need more than they already had. Most of them had favored giving up, had favored permitting the small ranchers to file homestead claims on strategic springs located on Pool range. Only he was holding on. He was the one who had influenced their vote. Without him they'd have given up.

What had already happened because of him was bad enough. Nothing more must happen for which he would have to feel responsible. The Stotts brothers must be taken alive. Care must be taken that none of the boys helping them were hurt.

He didn't know how many hours had passed since they'd stopped to eat and rest. But at last he heard the faint bawling of cattle from ahead.

He slowed and the men behind him slowed. Almost completely silent now, they went on until faintly in the distance they saw the red glow of a fire.

Foxworthy stopped, motionless and listening. He reasoned that if Floyd had stationed a guard, it would be back here from which direction any pursuit would come. Speaking as softly as he could, he said, "Hannigan, stay here. Don't go closer until it starts getting light. Albertson, stay with him."

To the others he said, "Johnson, you and Brown and Locke go right. I'll take Rider and Wills and go to the left. Stay out far enough so they can't hear your horses. When it gets light we'll move in on them. Eight of us ought to be able to keep any of them from getting away.

Just remember, there are only two grown men up there. The rest are boys. I don't want anybody shot."

"What if they shoot at us?"

Wearily, Foxworthy considered that. At last he said, "Shoot back. But not at boys. No matter what."

With Rider and Wills following, he rode out of the creek bottom onto the rolling plain. He held a steady course to the west for half a mile before he turned north again. Abreast of the fire, he said, "Stay here, Rider. Make yourself comfortable if you're sure you'll be awake as soon as it gets light."

"Don't worry. I always wake up at dawn. Besides, I doubt if I'll get much sleep tonight. It's too damn' cold."

Foxworthy went on, with Wills following. Three hundred yards farther on, he dropped Wills off. He went on for another three hundred yards himself, bearing right until he was slightly ahead of the rustlers in the bed of the creek.

What would he do, he asked himself, if Floyd or Russ came at him with guns firing? Would he be able to shoot them down?

To that question he had no answer for himself and he knew he would have none until the time for it actually came. He dismounted and tied his horse's reins to a clump of brush. He paced back and forth nervously, trying to keep warm but also trying to come to some kind of terms with himself.

Always before things had been clear for him. When someone tried to take something from you, you fought.

That lesson he had learned early when the Indians attacked the tiny cabin in which he and his father and mother lived. In the years since, the lesson had been impressed upon him many other times.

But now, with two good men dead because of a dead

cow and a dead calf, it didn't seem so important any more. Yet here he was, ready to once more take back something that had been taken away from him.

And not even from him personally, he thought ruefully. He had no interest in the cattle that belonged to the Cheyenne Pool. He was only a hired hand. He was forcing the members of the Pool to hold on and fight when they didn't really want to fight at all.

Yet he admitted that there was more to it than that. It was not the issue of stolen cattle, but of murder, the murder of Owens and his deputy.

His horse raised his head. Foxworthy hurried to him, suddenly aware that a breeze was blowing toward him from the rustlers' camp. The horse's ears were pricked toward the place. Foxworthy put one hand over the horse's nose and stroked his neck with the other. A horse whinnying out here would send the rustlers scattering in all directions and in the dark they'd probably all get away.

He began to pace back and forth again as soon as the breeze changed and the horse relaxed. The animal lowered his head and began to graze. For the moment he had lost the scent of the horses in the rustlers' camp, but he might pick it up again. Foxworthy stayed close in case he did.

He began to think of Lutie Mathias. She didn't need the Pool. She had land enough to run all the cattle that she owned. Nor, he thought, did he really need the Pool. An anachronism, a thing out of the past, it ought to be allowed to die. He had enough money saved to buy himself a place, to stock it adequately for a start. Let the Pool go. Let the small ranchers move in and take its land.

Once more the horse nervously raised his head. Quickly Foxworthy went to him and again clamped a hand over his nostrils.

The sky in the east was turning gray. A faint line along the horizon was visible. Another half to three quarters of an hour, Foxworthy thought, and it would be light enough.

What if the Stotts boys had guns? What if they opened fire on the men that had surrounded them?

Suddenly it dawned on Foxworthy that this could be a massacre. Not only Floyd and Russ were in danger of being killed, but so were the boys they had with them. And if anyone but Floyd or Russ was hurt he'd have an intolerable burden to square with himself.

Having made up his mind, he went quickly to his horse. Leading him, he moved softly and almost silently toward the rustlers' camp. The only way he could be sure those boys weren't going to get hurt would be to go in by himself. Only then could he be sure.

He wished he dared leave his horse behind but he did not. The horse might smell the camp again. He might give himself away. Foxworthy led him by holding to the bridle, ready to clamp a hand over his nostrils if it appeared to be necessary.

The horizon was now a lighter gray in the east. Gray was spreading slowly across the sky. Foxworthy reached the edge of the creek bed and stopped, breathing shallowly. For an instant he stood there motionless, trying to pierce the gloom with his glance. He saw the fire, saw several sleeping shapes nearby. He saw a man sitting on a dead down tree, puffing on a pipe. The man looked like Russ, but he could not be absolutely sure.

Where was Floyd? Was he one of the lumped shapes on the ground? Foxworthy knew Floyd was the deadly one. He'd wait as long as he dared to see if Floyd showed up. But when it was light enough for his men to attack, then he could wait no more.

The man at the fire knocked out his pipe and got to his feet. He stretched ponderously. Foxworthy could now see that it was, indeed, Russ. Russ put the dead pipe in his pocket and knelt to stir the fire up. Rising, he crossed to one of the sleeping shapes and stirred it with his toe. Foxworthy heard him say, "Come on, Floyd. Roll out."

The figure on the ground rolled and groaned. Foxworthy waited no more. Swiftly tying his horse, he withdrew the rifle from the saddle boot and carefully made his way down the cutbank and into the underbrush. It rustled with his passage but Floyd and Russ were talking now, and calling to the boys to get up and he didn't figure he would be heard.

Once he stopped, listening intently for the coming of the men he had left out there in the dark. He heard nothing, but by now it was light enough to clearly see objects a hundred yards away.

Cautiously, a careful step at a time, Foxworthy advanced. Finally, less than thirty feet away and concealed by a high clump of brush, he stopped. He drew his revolver and thumbed the hammer back.

It made a loud click, a foreign sound in this place and one that made both Floyd and Russ freeze motionless as they stood.

Softly, Foxworthy said, "It's over, boys. You're surrounded and you haven't got a chance. Just unbuckle your belts and let your guns slide to the ground. We found Owens and Kirby yesterday, so don't think we're going to hesitate."

And he held his breath a moment, waiting to see what they were going to do.

CHAPTER 14

He didn't have long to wait. Floyd literally exploded into action. He charged across the little clearing, straight at the nearest underbrush where Foxworthy was. Foxworthy's gun was ready, the hammer back, but he didn't shoot. Not for an instant. He was too taken by surprise.

And perhaps something else kept him from firing, some reluctance even he didn't completely understand. Perhaps he still felt vaguely guilty because he had started this by shooting the calf in Floyd Stotts' yard. In any event, Floyd managed to reach the cover of brush unharmed and dived into it not a dozen feet from where Foxworthy stood.

He heard the crash of breaking brush as Floyd plunged through it frantically. He yelled, "Russ, stand fast! You're surrounded!" Then turned and plunged through the underbrush after Floyd.

The possemen were coming now, yelling back and forth. Foxworthy could hear the pound of their galloping horses' hoofs. And suddenly he understood why Floyd had charged straight at him. Floyd had gambled that he wouldn't shoot, had gambled for his horse, saddled and ready, tied back in the underbrush.

Running hard but still short of the place he had tied the horse by a dozen yards, Foxworthy heard the distinctive slap as Floyd's rump hit the saddle. He heard the man yell and heard the sudden pound of the horse's hoofs. He saw the horse scramble up the steep cutbank out of the creek bed, his rider leaning forward and holding on, shoeless, hatless, shirttail flapping out behind. But Floyd was not unarmed. He had taken time to snatch his rifle up. It was now firmly clutched in his right hand.

Foxworthy turned his head and roared, "Somebody bring me a horse! Hurry up!" And then he stood, silent and motionless, watching the sheriff's killer ride away unscathed.

He should have fired when he had the chance, he told himself angrily. He could have brought Floyd down with a bullet in the legs. Or he could have killed him outright and saved the county the expense of a trial.

Yet somehow he wasn't sorry that he had not. Floyd had escaped and he would have to be run down and captured. But nobody could now say that Foxworthy, acting for the Cheyenne Pool, had tried, convicted, and executed him on the spot.

Wills rode up and Foxworthy said, "Get down and give me your horse. I'll catch up with Floyd. You and several of the others take Russ and those kids to town. Whoever is left can push the cattle back onto Pool range."

Without waiting for Wills's reply, he swung to the horse's back and thundered away. He heard a shout behind but didn't turn his head.

The horse lunged up the cutbank onto the level plain. In places there was partially frozen mud. In a few spots drifts of unmelted, dirty snow remained. Floyd had left a deeply indented trail but Foxworthy didn't have to follow trail. He could see his quarry less than half a mile away.

The temptation was great to spur his horse recklessly, to try and catch up at once. He resisted it. His own horse, which Floyd was riding, was a better horse than this one that he'd borrowed from Wills. He'd never close a half a mile distance. He'd only wear out his horse.

All he could do was keep Floyd in sight. Floyd had no boots, no coat, no hat. Before he'd gone ten miles he'd feel like he was frozen through. He'd *have* to stop and fight it out. Or he'd have to surrender himself.

Floyd was riding at a hard lope, so Foxworthy maintained an equal speed. An hour passed, and a strong, cold wind began to blow down out of the north.

Floyd now was heading toward a brushy canyon that lay between two flat-topped hills. Seeing his heading, Foxworthy felt like a lion hunter whose prey has suddenly gone up a tree. The chase was over before it hardly had begun. Floyd was cold and getting colder and he knew he had to stop and fight before he was too cold to shoot his gun.

Still half a mile ahead, Floyd disappeared into the canyon's rust-colored oakbrush. Foxworthy did not slow his pace. Holding his horse to a lope, he headed straight for the place where Floyd had disappeared. Meanwhile, his eyes roamed along the slopes on both sides of the canyon.

Either should give him a good view of canyon floor. And if there happened to be snow on the ground where the brush had protected it from the thawing sun, he'd be able to see Floyd easily. If Floyd decided not to stop, he'd know it and not waste time stalking him through the heavy brush.

Immediately he reined aside and began to climb the nearest slope, but he was halfway up before he could see down into the brush on the canyon floor.

He dragged his horse to a sudden halt. There was, indeed, a good covering of snow on the ground beneath the brush. He should be able to see Floyd, but he could not. A feeling of uneasiness came over him. He knew he had underestimated his enemy. Knowing that even now he might be too late, he flung himself from his horse.

The sound of the shot rolled flat and angry across the snow-speckled land. The bullet hit Foxworthy in the thigh, burning and fierce like the bite of a rattlesnake. But there was force to it too, force that felt like the blow of a fist or the kick of a mule. He fell wounded on the rocky slope where there was little or no cover. His horse, terrified by the sudden shot and by his rider's strange behavior, trotted away, not stopping until he had gone fifty yards.

Floyd had ambushed him, and wounded him, and Floyd would now finish him off as ruthlessly as he had finished off Owens and Kirby several days before. Floyd would then have the start he needed to get away. By the time a posse found Foxworthy's body and took up Floyd Stotts' trail, it would be too late. Snow would have covered it. And even if it had not, Floyd would at least have a start of several days.

Foxworthy's rifle was still in the saddle boot. He only had his revolver, which was useless at a range of more than fifty yards. And Floyd had that rifle, with which he was such an expert shot.

Foxworthy laid motionless, breathing very slowly and shallowly so that the motion of his body would not be discernible farther then fifty or a hundred feet away. He waited, with angry impatience, for his quarry to come to him.

Yet even as he waited, he knew his chances of getting Floyd were very slim. All Floyd had to do was stand back out of pistol range and pump him full of lead. With no risk whatever to himself.

His only hope, then, was to make Floyd believe that he was dead. That meant being completely motionless, no matter what happened, no matter what sounds came to his ears. He might hear the sound of Floyd jacking a cartridge into the chamber of his gun to replace the one expended, but he wouldn't dare move even though he believed Floyd was going to shoot again.

Now, despite the cold, he could feel sweat spring out on his forehead and upper lip. His wounded leg had begun to throb, its pain growing more excruciating with every minute that passed. He could feel the warm wetness of blood and wondered if Floyd's bullet had severed an artery. If it had, he'd lie here and bleed to death even if Floyd didn't bother to shoot him any more.

He heard the scuff of rock on rock down below him on the slope. He heard the rustle of dry leaves as Floyd came out of the heavy brush. He heard the sound of the lever on Floyd's rifle, the action opening and closing again. Despite all his efforts, his body grew tense and his nerves strained in anticipation of the bullet striking him.

But no sound came. He heard Floyd's voice call hoarsely, "Foxworthy? You son-of-a-bitch, are you shot dead?"

Lie still, he told himself. Don't breathe. Don't let a muscle twitch. If he sees movement or if he thinks he does, he'll put another bullet into you. Or if he sees the blood coming from your leg.

He heard another rock dislodged down on the slope. Floyd was barefooted so he wouldn't be making as much noise as would a man in boots. The man might be much closer than he had previously supposed. He might be coming fast up the slope, half frozen and scared, wanting to get on his horse and run but desperately needing both Foxworthy's horse and clothes.

Lying there, holding his breath with quiet desperation, Foxworthy squarely faced the prospect of his imminent death. He wondered what it would be like. A sudden darkness, he thought, and then an endless, dreamless sleep. He wondered if men did indeed live on after death, or if death was the end of everything.

He heard another rock stirred, and thought it was farther to one side than before. But why? Why would Floyd be circling?

The answer was there immediately. Floyd needed the horse for a spare. For some reason, perhaps because he had accepted the fact of Foxworthy's death, he was walking toward the horse, intending to catch him before stripping the clothes and boots from his dead enemy.

Still holding his breath, but feeling himself turning blue, Foxworthy waited a little longer, his muscles tensed like those of a cat before he springs. He heard the horse's hoofs grate against the rocks as the horse took several nervous steps away from Floyd.

"Now!" he said to himself. "Now, before he reaches the horse, before he's close enough to duck behind the horse."

His tense and gathered muscles brought him rolling over, brought him awkwardly but swiftly to his knees. His gun, drawn from its holster and cocked as it cleared, now leveled itself, pointing in the direction of the horse. Foxworthy's voice roared hoarsely, "Hold it, Floyd! I'll kill you if you try to turn!"

Floyd's back was toward him. The man was less than six feet from the horse, his left hand outstretched coaxingly. The rifle was in his right hand, dangling at his side. Floyd froze in this position and a bitter curse escaped his lips.

He turned his head. For a long moment he stared at Foxworthy there on his knees. Then he said, "You was hit, wasn't you? You wasn't just puttin' on."

Foxworthy said, "I was hit. But I'm a long damn' ways from dead."

"What you goin' to do, now you got the drop on me?"

Foxworthy said, "Drop the gun. Then back away up the hill from it."

"And if I won't?"

"I can kill you, Floyd."

Floyd shrugged. "All right. But you're makin' a mistake. You've lost a lot of blood. You'll lose a lot more before we get to town. And you know what I'll do to you if you pass out."

Foxworthy repeated, "Drop the gun."

Floyd studied him speculatively, making no move to obey. Finally he said, "Tell you what I'll do. Let me go an' I'll just ride away. I'll leave you your horse."

Foxworthy shook his head, knowing as he did that he was a fool not to take Floyd up on it. The chances of his hanging onto consciousness until he got Floyd back to town were slim. So were the chances that he'd find any of the other men where he had left them, or that he'd be able to catch up with the cattle and their drovers before he passed out from loss of blood.

Then he thought of Kirby and of Owens, killed by Floyd and covered with earth as if they'd been dogs instead of men. He shook his head and when his voice came this time it had an edge to it for all that it was weaker than before. "Drop it or I'll put a slug in you!"

Floyd studied his face closely for a moment more. Then, reluctantly, he released the rifle and let it clatter to the ground.

Foxworthy said, "Now, back on up the hill. Forty or fifty feet. Move, damn you!"

"You won't shoot."

"By God, don't you count on that!"

Floyd backed slowly up the hill, watching Foxworthy with bright and calculating eyes. When he was twenty-five feet from the rifle, Foxworthy forced himself to his feet. Limping painfully and nearly falling at every step, he walked toward it.

Floyd stood poised above him, eyes hastily searching the slope nearby for a rock big enough to throw. Foxworthy reached the gun. He stooped to pick it up.

His leg gave way and he fell forward just as Floyd snatched a rock from the ground and flung it down the hill at him.

The rock whistled harmlessly over his head. He recovered the rifle. Using it as a crutch, he came upright and with his revolver put a bullet into the ground at Floyd's bare feet. He said, "Go catch my horse."

Floyd picked his way down the slope toward Foxworthy's horse. Foxworthy fished a knife out of his pocket. He slit his pants leg over the bullet hole and then ripped it back to expose the wound.

The wound was bleeding profusely where the bullet had exited, but it was bleeding steadily and not in spurts. It would probably stop eventually by itself. All he had to do was stay conscious until he got help or until he got to town with Floyd.

CHAPTER 15

Floyd got Foxworthy's horse and led the animal toward him. When he was still ten feet away, Foxworthy said, "That's far enough. Step back away from him."

Floyd backed away, studying him, gauging his weakness carefully. Foxworthy limped to his horse. Reaching him, he flung Floyd's rifle down the hill into the brush. Floyd protested, "Hey! That's mine!"

"You won't be needing it. Not where you're going."

"You got no right . . ."

"Don't talk rights to me, you son-of-a-bitch!" Foxworthy said savagely.

It was Foxworthy's left leg that was wounded and he wasn't sure he could mount. Gritting his teeth, he stooped. He lifted his left foot with both hands and placed it in the stirrup. Then, using both hands on the saddle horn, he pulled himself into the saddle, hitting it dizzy, sweating, and weak.

He looked at Floyd. "Where's my horse at?"

"Down there in the brush."

"Get him. I'll be right behind. Try anything and I'll cripple you the way you crippled me."

Floyd walked down the hill. Foxworthy stayed close behind. They entered the heavy brush. Floyd pushed his way through, deliberately releasing the branches he had pushed aside in such a way that they struck either Foxworthy's horse or Foxworthy himself. But Foxworthy didn't fall back because he didn't dare. If he let Floyd out of his sight, the man would get away.

Floyd reached his horse and untied him. Still bare-footed, he mounted and headed out through the heaviest of the brush. Foxworthy followed without complaint. They reached the edge of the brush and rode out into open country. Here, Foxworthy hesitated briefly between heading back to where he had left the other men, trying to intercept the herd, or heading straight for town.

Because of the uncertainty of the first two choices, he chose to head straight for town, even though he knew he could never reach it today. He got Floyd lined out in the right direction and afterward let himself relax, concentrating only on staying close enough behind Floyd so that the man wouldn't be tempted to try and get away.

He glanced down at his leg. It was still bleeding, but not as much as it had before. The blood had begun to clot.

Foxworthy had never been one for self-examination. But suddenly he could not avoid looking at himself any longer. He stood at a crossroads, he realized. And he admitted something he could never have admitted to himself before today. He had avoided human relationships because he was afraid of them, because he distrusted them. He had, instead, given his loyalty to employers, who, for the most part, used it the same way they used him.

Floyd glanced over his shoulder and met Foxworthy's glance. Foxworthy growled, "I'm still all right, if that's what you're wondering."

Floyd said, "I can wait." He turned his head again. Deliberately he urged his horse to trot, knowing what that uneven, jolting gait would do to Foxworthy's wounded leg.

Foxworthy's horse matched the trot of the other horse until Foxworthy hauled him in. He called, "Pull back, damn you, unless you want me to shoot."

Floyd pulled his horse back to a walk again. And Foxworthy understood that this was to be his strategy. He'd try to wear his captor down, weaken him, hurt him as much as possible. He knew that sooner or later pain and loss of blood would tell.

The hours dragged. Clouds obscured the sun, so neither man realized exactly when it set. But gray deepened in the sky and at last Foxworthy called a halt. They stopped in a little draw, where a drift of snow remained that could be melted for water for them to drink.

Foxworthy waited until Floyd had dismounted. Then he swung painfully to the ground himself.

His leg had stiffened, and would not support his weight. He withdrew his rifle from the boot and used it for a crutch. Balancing himself precariously, he tied Floyd's horse and then his own. Glancing at Floyd, he said, "Gather some wood and build a fire."

"You go to hell."

Foxworthy drew his revolver and thumbed the hammer back. He raised the gun and sighted it on Floyd's right knee. He tightened his finger slowly, carefully.

Floyd stood it for only a couple of seconds before he yelled, "All right! I'll do it!"

Foxworthy didn't lower the gun. "Then do it. And don't get out of my sight."

Floyd was staring at him. "You son-of-a-bitch, you'd have done it, wouldn't you?"

"I'd have done it."

Floyd stared at him an instant more, then he turned and shuffled away. There was not much wood, only a few dead branches on half a dozen scrubby trees. Floyd broke them off one by one and then returned with an armload of them. He knelt and began breaking off the smaller twigs, building to larger ones. He fumbled for a match and lit the pile. The fire grew and made Foxworthy realize how chilled his leg was and how numb. He stood as close to the fire as he could, soaking up its heat. When he had warmed himself a little he said, "There's some grub behind my saddle. Get it and start cooking it."

Floyd got the sack from behind the saddle of Foxworthy's horse. There was a coffeepot which he filled with snow and put on to heat. There was a pan and a slab of bacon, which he sliced with his knife.

Foxworthy waited until bacon and coffee were on the fire. Then he said, "Get the saddles off."

Sullenly Floyd moved to obey. He tossed them on the ground and started to untie the horses. Foxworthy said, "We won't picket them. They can stand a day without food."

Floyd returned to the fire. Foxworthy dragged his own saddle closer to the fire and eased himself down on it. He stretched his leg out, noticing that it had begun to bleed again.

There was also some bread in the sack. After wrapping some strips of blanket around his feet, Floyd sliced it and fried the slices in the bacon grease. He helped himself, ignoring Foxworthy, until Foxworthy said, "I'll take that plate. You get another one."

Sullenly Floyd handed the plate to him. He plainly was considering trying to kick Foxworthy in the head as he stepped back. Foxworthy's steady glance made him change his mind.

Foxworthy waited until Floyd sat down. Then he ate, even though the food made him feel sicker than he already was. He drank the coffee, pleased to realize that eating had improved the way he felt.

But he knew he wasn't going to get through the night unless Floyd was tied. And he further knew Floyd would never allow himself to be tied.

Foxworthy laid aside his plate and cup. He struggled to his feet. He picked up his cup and headed for the fire, as if to refill it.

He walked behind Floyd, as if wary of the man. He saw Floyd's half smile even as he drew his gun. Floyd saw the motion too, and started to turn his head. Foxworthy brought the gun barrel down in a swiftly savage arc. It struck the top of Floyd's head with an audible crack and Floyd collapsed forward and laid still.

Foxworthy holstered the gun. Limping painfully, he tore strips from the same blanket Floyd had used to wrap his feet. He tied them together and, pulling Floyd's hands behind his back, he bound them as tightly as he could. He then brought Floyd's feet up close to the hands and tied them together and to the bound hands. After that he got his rope from his saddle and trussed Floyd securely around and around with that, after which he tied the end securely to the base of a scrubby tree. By the time he had finished he was weak and dizzy. He got a blanket from behind the saddle of the horse he had borrowed and laid it over Floyd. He got another for himself and laid down on the ground, as close to the fire as he dared to be.

Floyd groaned and stirred. When he opened his eyes, they were virulent and savage but they held neither mockery nor certainty any more. He glared at Foxworthy and Foxworthy said, "What the hell did you expect? If I hadn't hit you, you'd have put up a fight. And you'd have won."

"I'll kill you if it's the last thing I ever do."

"Sure. Only first you've got to get a chance."

He closed his eyes. The world seemed to whirl crazily for a moment, and then he fell asleep.

Floyd Stotts awakened him, thrashing furiously around, trying to get loose. He got up, rebuilt the fire, and by its light, examined Floyd's bonds. They had loosened slightly from his thrashing, but they were still tight enough. Foxworthy dragged his gold watch out of his pocket and glanced at it. It had stopped and he had no idea what time it was. He put it back into his pocket without rewinding it.

He laid down again, surprised that he felt better even though his leg was stiffer and more painful than before. He didn't go back to sleep, but lay staring up at the black and starless sky. Floyd said, his teeth chattering, "Jesus it's cold. You tie a man so goddam tight his blood can't circulate."

Foxworthy didn't bother to reply. Maybe he was light-headed from his wound, but he had come to a decision. When he got back to town he was going to quit the Cheyenne Pool.

He closed his eyes, but he didn't go to sleep. He'd ask Lutie Mathias to marry him. The Cheyenne Pool was finished anyway. When men lose the will to fight for what they have, then they are easy prey for wolves.

Dawn touched the sky with gray. Foxworthy got up and unwound the lariat from Floyd. With his knife he slashed enough of the blanket bindings so that Floyd could work himself loose. Then he stepped back and waited until he had.

Floyd got up, staggering, and began flinging his arms around trying to restore their circulation. He jumped up and down until blood was running in his legs again. After allowing him enough time to get his circulation going again, Foxworthy said, "Saddle the horses. Mine first."

Floyd turned his head and glared, but he moved sullenly to obey. When his horse was saddled, Foxworthy mounted the same way he had yesterday. Only when he was in the saddle did he say, "Now yours."

Floyd saddled the horse he had been riding yesterday. Foxworthy said, "Move out."

Scowling, Floyd rode out. Foxworthy grinned grimly to himself. Yesterday Floyd had been sure of overcoming him. He had been sure of an opportunity to escape. Now he wasn't sure. He didn't even have much hope.

At a walk, they made their way steadily toward town. In midafternoon they rode into it.

A crowd gathered and followed them to the jail, jabbering excitedly. Several men took Floyd inside and locked him in a cell. A couple of others volunteered to stay there on guard.

Foxworthy headed up the street toward the doctor's house, weaker than he had ever felt before.

He got halfway before he swayed, toppled and fell out of the saddle onto the frozen street. They carried him the rest of the way to the doctor's house and left him on Doc's old leather couch. Muttering to himself, Doc went to work on him.

CHAPTER 16

When Foxworthy regained consciousness, he was lying on Dr. Wilcox's couch. The leg of his pants had been cut away and his thigh bandaged. The wound hurt like hell. He grimaced with the pain and Doc Wilcox said, "Here, drink this."

"What is it?"

"Laudanum. It'll ease the pain."

"Make me groggy too, won't it?"

"A little."

Foxworthy growled, "To hell with it. I can stand the pain." He swung his legs over the side of Doc's leather couch and sat up. His head reeled and he steadied himself with both hands on the couch. Doc asked, "What do you think you're doing?"

"I'm leaving. You've done your work. Now I'll do mine."

Doc turned his head and called, "Miss Mathias!"

She came from the parlor into Doc's cluttered office. Doc said, "You talk to him. He says he's leaving."

Lutie's eyes showed her worry. They also showed relief that he was conscious and able to sit up. She said, "The doctor wants you to stay here overnight."

Foxworthy shook his head.

"Why, for heaven's sake?"

"Too much to do."

"There's nothing that can't wait."

"Nothing that can't wait? Pool riders are camped out

on the springs right now, trying to hold onto them. And what do you think Floyd's family and friends are going to do when they find out he and Russ are in jail?"

"Someone else can take care of it. You're hurt."

He shook his head, which now had cleared. He pushed himself to his feet, conscious of his bare, hairy leg below the bandages. He said to Doc, "Did you have to ruin a good pair of pants?"

Doc said disgustedly, "Oh for God's sake! Get out of here. I'll send you a bill." He opened a closet door and took out a cane. "Bring it back when you're through with it."

Lutie asked worriedly, "Is it safe for him to leave?"

"Well, he might tear those stitches out and start bleeding again. Or he might pass out. But if he's as tough as he is stubborn, he'll be all right."

Foxworthy limped to the door, using the cane. His head was reeling again but he wasn't going to admit it, either to Lutie or to Doc. Lutie helped him into his coat and handed him his hat. As they stepped out into the cold, late afternoon wind, she said, "The members of the Pool are meeting at the hotel."

"What for?"

"I guess they want to throw in the sponge."

"And you?"

"I guess I don't want anybody else getting killed. Not for land that doesn't even belong to us."

Coming in with Floyd, he had decided to quit the Pool. He'd decided to ask the county commissioners to appoint him to finish out Ray Owens's term. Now, suddenly, he realized that was impossible. If he quit the Pool, it would be a surrender and the small ranchers would know it was. It would be open season not only on land held by the Pool but on their cattle too and even if he was sheriff he couldn't hold them back. Not by himself. He said, "I was going to quit, but I can't. Not now. Not with things the way they are."

"Is pride that important to you?"

He stopped and, leaning on the cane, looked down at her. "Is that what you think it is?"

"Isn't it?" Her glance was searching but he met it steadily.

He said, "No. It isn't pride. I guess it's just trying to do what's right."

"They don't appreciate what you're trying to do. They want you to quit. They're up there in the hotel right now voting to fire you."

Unexpectedly he grinned at her. "Won't do 'em any good. I'm not going to quit. I owe that much to Ray."

"To Ray? Ray is dead."

"And others will be too if the Pool pulls back off that range. You don't seriously think for a minute that the Stottses and their friends will divide it peacefully, do you?"

"Is the alternative for the Pool to keep on holding it?"

"For now it is. Until things cool down."

She hesitated and he said, "Come on, let's get up to the hotel and see what's going on."

Limping, leaning heavily on the cane Doc had given him, he headed for the hotel. Lutie walked beside him, white-faced and worried. They found the members of the Pool in the hotel dining room. Foxworthy followed Lutie in and demanded, "What's going on?"

Meyer Garth answered him. "This has gone too far, Dan. Ray and Tom Kirby are dead. We want to quit before somebody else gets killed."

Foxworthy scowled at him. "Do you know what will happen if you withdraw from all that range?"

"They'll move in and take it, I suppose. But we can ship the cattle. Even if we take a loss, it will be better than more men getting killed. Ray Owens was my friend. So was Tom Kirby."

Foxworthy laughed harshly. "And you think they'll divide up three hundred square miles of range peacefully? Hell, they'll be fightin' over it like starvin' dogs over a bone."

"You don't know that."

"And you don't know they'll split it up peacefully. Or that they'll be satisfied with just the land. I figure they'll take the cattle too. And whoever tries to stop them will get what Owens and Kirby got."

Garth said stubbornly, "We've made up our minds. We've voted to pull back."

Foxworthy's face reddened. He said harshly, "Well by God, you can vote until hell freezes over. I'm not pulling back. The crew is camped out on those springs where I sent them. And they're going to stay."

"Pull them back. Or we will."

"Who's we? All of you?"

Garth nodded. "It was unanimous."

"And if I say no?"

"We discussed that too. We're letting you go, Dan, if you refuse to do what we tell you to."

Dan stared at him incredulously. "Well by God, mister, I won't quit! What the hell do you think of that?"

Garth said weakly, "Your pay stops today."

Foxworthy laughed. "Then I'll work without any pay."

"We'll get somebody to replace you. We'll make you quit."

Foxworthy glared at him. "Do that, Mister Garth. Do that. In the meantime, I'm running the Pool just like I always have. And the Pool is holding onto its land."

Garth stared at him confusedly for a moment. At last he said, "If anything happens, it's your responsibility. We won't stand back of you."

"But you'll accept the benefits of whatever I do, won't you? Just like you always have."

He turned and limped angrily from the room. Lutie followed him. There was silence behind them until they were halfway across the lobby. Then everyone in the dining room began to talk at once.

Outside, Lutie said, "Dan, why won't you quit? You're not responsible for the whole community."

He paused a moment, leaning on the cane. Thoughtfully he said, "I guess maybe that's what's bothering me. I've spent my life worrying just about myself. Or about whoever I happened to be working for. But when we dug up Ray and Tom out there where Floyd and Russ buried them like a couple of dogs, I realized that it was because of me that they were dead."

"That isn't so. It was because of Floyd and Russ Stotts and their greed that Ray and Tom were killed."

"That's what I tried to tell myself. That's the way I tried to get myself off the hook. Only I knew it wasn't true. And I knew I couldn't quit."

"Are you sure you're right?"

He grinned ruefully. "No. I'm not sure at all. First I decided I'd quit the Pool and get the county commissioners to appoint me to finish out Ray's term. But then I realized that the minute I quit the Pool, all that land would be up for grabs. Even if I was sheriff, I couldn't stop it because I'd be just one man against them all. As foreman of the Pool, I've got fifty men to hold them off and that's the kind of muscle they understand."

"So what are you going to do now?"

"Find out if that wagon has gone back out to Lance

McFee. If it hasn't, I want to send him word to come on back to town."

"So he can register homestead claims for the Pool?"

He nodded.

"And then?"

"Why I guess I'll spend the night at the jail."

"You don't have to do that. You can get a room at the hotel."

He nodded. "All right. I'll give that much. I do feel poorly and that's the truth."

"Do you want something to eat?"

"Uh huh. But first I want a drink, and I want to buy a pair of pants. Tell you what. I'll meet you back at the hotel in an hour."

She nodded doubtfully. Foxworthy left her standing on the windswept sidewalk and headed for Holloman's Mercantile, hurrying to get there before it closed. He bought a pair of pants, which he had difficulty getting on over the bandages. He told the youthful clerk at the store to throw the old ones away, then went out again into the wind.

He walked down the street to the Red Dog Saloon. There was a good crowd inside, some of them men who had been with Foxworthy when the bodies of Owens and Kirby had been found. He limped to the bar and ordered a drink.

Men crowded around him, sympathizing with him about his wounded leg, congratulating him on catching the killers of the sheriff and his deputy. Foxworthy gulped his drink and poured another one. Carrying the bottle, he walked to a table and sat down. Several men followed him, among them Theodore Dodd, who had ridden to Lance McFee's soddy after the buckboard with which to bring back the bodies of Owens and Kirby. Foxworthy asked, "You take that buckboard back out to McFee?"

The man shook his head. "I guess I forgot, what with all the excitement and everything."

"Is Hannigan still in town?"

"Was, a while ago. I saw him down at Garcia's Restaurant."

"Mind finding him? Tell him to take the buckboard back and give McFee a message to come on back to town. Tell him I said so."

"Sure, Dan. Right away." The man hurried out of the saloon and turned toward Garcia's Restaurant.

Dan leaned back in his chair and gulped another drink. The pain in his leg was lessening, and a pleasant drowsiness was stealing over him. He wished he could sleep right now, but he knew it was impossible. He still had to check the jail and make sure there were at least two tough and reliable men on guard. After that, he'd have supper with Lutie and after that he would have to go see Tom Kirby's wife.

He laid a half dollar on the table and got to his feet. He limped out into the gathering dusk and headed for the jail.

Two men were there, Rider and Chet Wills. Both had been with him on the chase after Floyd and Russ. He limped inside and sat down painfully in the sheriff's swivel chair. "Everything all right?"

"Sure. Why wouldn't it be?"

"Eaten yet?"

Rider shook his head. "I was just getting ready to go."

"Go ahead. I'll stay here until you get back. Just bring four trays. You can eat back here."

"Why?"

"Two men ought to be here all the time and I can't stay."

"You think somebody might try to break Floyd an' Russ out of jail?"

"I don't think so. But it's a possibility."

Rider got up and went out the door. Wills closed it and bolted it. Foxworthy settled down to wait until Rider got back with the trays, satisfied that the two were alerted sufficiently. Out in back, Floyd Stotts began to yell, demanding his supper. Neither Wills nor Foxworthy bothered to answer him.

CHAPTER 17

Rider was back in twenty minutes, carrying four dinner trays. He kicked on the door and Wills admitted him, immediately taking two of the trays from him. Foxworthy said, "See you later," and went out into the street, which now was dark. He walked uptown to the hotel.

Lutie was waiting in one of the lobby chairs. She got up when he came in, smiling approval at the new trousers he had on. She noted how tight they were over the bandage and asked, "Does it hurt?"

He grinned. "It hurts."

"I guess that was a silly question."

"It was. Let's go in and eat."

He followed her into the diningroom and across it to a small table by a window looking into the street. He sat down facing her. She asked, "What now?"

"Tonight, you mean? I've got to go see Tom Kirby's wife."

"No. I meant tomorrow. And the day after that."

"We file on those springs. Floyd and Russ go to trial. Next fall, you and the other Pool members can sell your cattle and after that it won't matter what happens to your range."

"Do you really think it's going to be as easy as you say?"

He grinned ruefully. "No. It won't be that easy. That's just the way I hope it goes."

"Do you think the small ranchers will make trouble?"

"There's less chance of it with Floyd in jail."

That seemed to satisfy her. Their dinner came, and they ate in virtual silence. There was something Dan wanted to say to her but he couldn't seem to get it phrased right in his mind. As they were finishing, he finally said, "I'm still going to try and get the sheriff's job. Once the matter of the springs is settled and Floyd and Russ have been tried, anybody can ramrod the Pool."

Lutie looked at him, a question in her eyes. He said, "I want you to marry me."

Her glance met his steadily. "Do you really think we can get along?" She didn't know how he was going to take that, and was surprised when he grinned at her disarmingly. He said, "Sure we can. I wasn't planning to treat you like I treat Floyd Stotts."

She had to smile at that. She studied him thoughtfully for a moment before she said candidly, "I'll marry you. I have known you were going to ask and I have already thought about it. I am not so sure about us, but then nothing in life is sure, is it?"

"No. Nothing is sure." His face was solemn now and his eyes were very serious. "You won't regret it. I will be very good to you."

She put out a hand and covered his with it. "And I will be very good to you."

At one in the morning, a shadowy group of men tied their horses in a little grove of trees two blocks from the jail. Theron Stotts, leading them, said, "Jake, you and Frank and Bill stay here and hold the horses. You hear shootin', you come a runnin' with them. Understand?"

Jake Samuels grunted agreement. Theron said, "All right, the rest of you come along. I don't want no shootin' if it can be helped. But we're gettin' Floyd an' Russ out of that goddam jail."

Walking quietly, in the middle of the street, the group headed uptown toward the jail. There were twelve of them now that three had been left behind.

The town slept. Even the saloon was closed. There was a single light in a second-story window of the hotel, but otherwise the town was completely dark. At the jail, the group paused. Theron whispered, "Three or four go around in back. The rest of you come with me."

He crossed the boardwalk to the door of the jail, walking on his toes so as not to make any noise. He waited until those with him had taken positions on both sides of the door. Then he knocked lightly.

There was no answer. Theron knocked again, more loudly than before.

This time a protesting, sleepy voice answered from inside, "Who the hell is that? What do you want?"

"Foxworthy sent me. Open up."

Light flickered in the jail windows as someone inside lighted a lamp. The doorbolt shot back and the door opened just a crack.

Theron hit it with his shoulder. It slammed against the man inside, flinging him back. Pushing the door wide, Theron leaped through, a shotgun in his hands. Behind him, the others crowded in. Some carried shotguns, some rifles. One man, who owned no gun, had a pitchfork in his hands.

Rider was sprawled out helplessly on the floor. Wills sat up on the cot and reached for his gun lying beside him on the floor. Theron yelled, "Let it alone!" but Wills was too sleepy and too startled to instantly obey. He got his hand on the gun and raised it, thumbing the hammer back.

Belatedly, he realized what he had done. He dropped the gun and tried to raise his hands, but it was too late. The shotgun in Theron's hands roared, then roared again as the second barrel discharged immediately on the heels of the first.

The first charge of birdshot took Wills in the chest, opening up a raw and gory hole as big as a man's fist. Tearing on through, the charge spattered blood and shredded flesh on the wall behind the cot.

The second charge coming from a muzzle forced upward slightly by the first, took Wills in the throat and literally severed his head. Hanging only by a thin strand of flesh and skin, it fell shockingly to one side. Mercifully, Wills was that way for only a split second before his whole upper body toppled back to the floor behind the cot.

Rider stared in horror from the floor. So did the men with Theron, and his brothers, Sam and Hal. Motionless, Theron held the smoking shotgun, as startled as the others by what he just had done. He had fired from reflex because Wills had snatched up his gun. He hadn't meant to kill the man, but he had, and he knew with a sick, empty feeling in his belly that there could now be no going back. Not for him any more than for Floyd and Russ. All three were murderers and if they went to trial, they'd hang. A man said in a shocked, almost inaudible voice, "What the hell did you do that for? He'd dropped his goddam gun!"

Theron swung his head, eyes blazing furiously. "You son-of-a-bitch, he was tryin' to shoot me! All I done was defend myself!" He looked at the other men. "You saw it! You saw him grab up that gun! What was I supposed to do, stand here and let the bastard kill me?"

The man repeated, "He'd dropped the gun."

Theron rushed at him, swinging the shotgun like a club.

It connected with the man's shoulder and knocked him three feet to one side.

The others grabbed Theron from behind. "Stop it! This ain't goin' to help. What's done is done."

Theron controlled himself with a visible effort. He shook off their hands. He said, "That's right. What's done is done. Let's get Floyd and Russ an' get out of here." He crossed to the sheriff's desk and picked up the keys from it. He turned and gave the keys to Hal. "Get 'em out. And hurry. Them gunshots will bring the whole damn' town!"

Hal hurried through the door leading to the cells. Rider remained on the floor, his eyes shocked and horrified, plainly afraid to move lest he get the same treatment Wills had got.

Hal returned, with Floyd and Russ. Floyd looked at Wills's bloody, crumpled body, and Theron said, "I had to. The son-of-a-bitch had a gun on me."

Floyd took over the leadership of the group immediately. He said, "Let's get going! Where are the horses?"

"We left 'em a couple of blocks from here. Jake was to bring 'em the minute he heard shots."

Floyd stepped out into the street, following the others. There now were several lights showing in the windows of the hotel. Up the street a man's voice yelled, "Hey! what the hell is going on?"

Floyd bawled, "Nothin'! Go back to bed!"

An upstairs window in the hotel slammed open and a man leaned out, a revolver in his hand. He opened fire on the group in the street, aiming carefully and spacing his shots. He hit one of the men down in the street and the man fell, yelling with the pain of his wound. Floyd bawled, "It's Foxworthy! Kill the son-of-a-bitch!"

Shots now racketed in the street as the small ranchers opened fire on the man in the hotel. The shotgun blasts were wasted but they made a lot of noise. One of the rifle bullets shattered the window over Foxworthy's head and showered him with glass. He pulled back, already reloading his gun as he did.

Floyd roared, "The horses! Get to the horses!"

As if in answer to his shout, Jake and the two who had stayed with him came galloping up the street, each towing several riderless horses behind. The men ran for their horses, mounted and raced back down the street, even as Foxworthy opened up again from the hotel. One of the horses, hit, began to buck. His rider sailed off, laid in the street stunned for a moment, then ran and caught up with one of his comrades. The man gave him a stirrup and he swung up behind. In a minute more the street was empty save for the still-bucking horse and the wounded man lying groaning in the middle of the street.

Rider came running from the jail. Foxworthy came limping down the street, surrounded by excited townspeople, all talking and shouting at once. Rider saw Foxworthy and yelled, "Dan! They killed Wills! And they got Floyd and Russ!"

Foxworthy reached the jail. He went in, followed by Rider and by townspeople who jammed the door. Seeing what had once been Wills, the townspeople pushed back out. One man ran around the corner of the building and began throwing up.

Foxworthy stared at Wills, his own stomach churning. He'd seen men like this before during the war, but that had been a long time ago. Rider said in a small, shocked voice, "He'd dropped his gun and started to put up his hands but that son-of-a-bitch Theron let him have both barrels anyway. The first took him in the chest and the second goddam near took his head clear off. Holy God, Dan, it was an awful thing to see!"

Foxworthy looked at him. "You got names?"

"Damn' right I got names. I can name every man who came in here."

"There's paper and pencil on the desk. Write out a statement and write down the names."

"What are you going to do?"

"Get warrants for every damn one of them. Get the commissioners to appoint me deputy. Get a posse and go after them."

Rider crossed to the desk. He sat down, found paper and pencil and began to write. Foxworthy went to the door. There still was a cluster of half-dressed, excited townspeople in the street. Foxworthy said, "I want a posse ready to go as soon as it is light. I can use every man I can get. Have horses, rifles, grub, and blankets."

The men scattered, talking excitedly. Dan turned and waited impatiently until Rider had finished writing. He picked up the paper. There were nine names on the sheet, including those of Theron, Sam, and Hal Stotts. He said, "Go home and get your horse if you want to go after them with me."

"I want to go."

"We'll meet at daylight here."

Rider stumbled up the street toward home. Foxworthy limped toward Judge Foster's house.

There was a light burning in the judge's parlor, and another one upstairs. Foxworthy knocked. The judge answered the door, clad in a nightshirt. Foxworthy said, "They broke Floyd and Russ out of jail. They killed Wills." He handed Rider's statement to the judge. "I want warrants for every one of those. I'll get as many of the commissioners together as I can and get myself appointed deputy."

The judge glanced at the paper. "I'll have the warrants ready when you get back."

Foxworthy limped away. He made it as far as Phil Hackett's house before his leg gave out. He sank on Hackett's red velvet sofa and said, "I'll go after them if you'll get the commissioners together and appoint me to take Owens's place."

Hackett got him a bottle and glass before he left. Foxworthy sat exhausted on the sofa and poured himself a drink. Hackett's three children peered curiously at him from the doorway until their mother shooed them back upstairs to bed. She came in and sat down and tried uncomfortably to carry on a conversation that did not touch on the tragedy.

Foxworthy poured himself another drink. He was too tired even to wonder if Wills's death was not another to be charged to the calf-killing episode.

CHAPTER 18

Hackett was back in an hour. He said, "You're now the new sheriff, appointed to fill out Owens's term. But what about the Pool?"

"They can't last and they know it."

"And the springs?"

"The Pool would give up the springs if the small ranchers would agree to let them keep their cattle on that range until they can liquidate next fall."

"Will they?" Hackett stared at him as if he had never thought he'd hear such words of compromise from the man who spoke for the Cheyenne Pool.

Foxworthy nodded. "Without the Stotts brothers to stir them up, I think they will."

Hackett heaved a sigh. "Then maybe this trouble is over with."

"Not until we catch Floyd and Russ and the men who helped break them out of jail."

"When are you leaving?"

Foxworthy limped to the door. "As soon as it gets light." He was sick and weak and he didn't know whether he had the strength for a day-long ride. But he knew he had to try. He thanked Hackett, went out the door, and headed toward the jail.

Already there was a thin long line of gray along the horizon in the east. There were about a dozen men, with horses, waiting at the jail.

Someone had carried Chet Wills's body to the undertaker's, but the blood and bits of flesh plastered on the wall and floor had not been cleaned up. Foxworthy tried to ignore sight of them as he went into the office and sank into the sheriff's swivel chair.

Outside, the sky grew lighter. More men arrived, excited and nervous.

Judge Foster came with the warrants. There were eleven, counting those for Floyd and Russ. Foxworthy called one of the men in and asked him to go to the livery barn and get him a horse. "I think my saddle's down there, but if you can't find it, get any saddle you can find."

The man left. Out in the street, the possemen were shivering, talking among themselves, glancing impatiently in through the windows. Hannigan came in, eyes red, face slack from a night of drinking. Foxworthy asked, "Feel like going along?"

Hannigan grimaced. "I'll bet I feel a lot better than you do."

The man Foxworthy had sent to the livery stable for a horse came riding back leading a big sorrel with Foxworthy's saddle on. Foxworthy got reluctantly to his feet. He limped to the door, using the cane.

His rifle was still in the saddle boot. He mounted painfully, then shoved the cane down into the boot with the rifle.

The others had mounted and were looking at him expectantly. He said, "We'll go to Indian Springs."

"Why not Stotts' place? Hell, that's where they'll all go."

"Maybe. But there are a lot of women and kids out there. I don't want to drag them into it if it can be helped." He started down the street, turned for an instant to look toward the hotel. A group of people stood in front, looking after the departing posse. Lutie Mathias was one of them.

Foxworthy said, "Go on. I'll catch up," and rode back up the street to the hotel.

Lutie came out into the frozen street and looked up at him. "How do you feel?"

"Rotten." He grinned down at her. "But I'll live."

"I wish you didn't have to go."

"I know. But I started this, I guess, and it's up to me to finish it."

"You didn't start it. Floyd Stotts' greed is what started it. And there were plenty out there willing to go along with him."

He nodded. "Goodbye."

"That sounds so final." She made a determined smile. "Don't think you're going to get out of marrying me that easily."

He reached down and took her hand. It was cold, but it gripped his and held on almost desperately. He said, "Tonight. I'll see you tonight."

She released his hand, nodding. There was a brightness in her eyes that had not been there a moment ago. Foxworthy turned his horse and lifted him to a lope. The gait hurt him so badly he had to hold onto the saddle horn but he didn't pull back. He had to catch up with the posse. He didn't trust them to go on alone. All the men in the posse had known Ray and Tom and Chet.

A half mile from town he caught up with them. One man asked, "Why the hell can't we go out to the Stotts' place? It'll sure save us a lot of time."

"I told you why." Foxworthy left the road, cutting straight across country toward Indian Springs. Floyd and Russ and Theron would be planning to leave the country.

But he figured that before they left, they'd seize Indian Springs. They had already paid too heavy a price to leave without getting it.

Theron Stotts was white and shaken as he mounted his horse and rode out of town, following Floyd, who was in the lead.

He had not meant to kill Chet Wills. He was desperately sorry it had happened. He had known Chet fairly well, having played poker with him a few times, and talked casually with him almost every time he came to town.

He looked at Floyd's broad back, just a darker spot in the darkness ahead of him. All this was Floyd's fault, he thought. It had been Floyd's idea to kill Pool cows so that their calves could be stolen without risk. It had been Floyd's idea to seize Indian Springs. It had been Floyd's idea to steal a herd of Pool cattle and Floyd had been the one who had murdered Ray Owens and Tom Kirby.

Furthermore, Floyd was responsible for the fact that he had killed Chet Wills just a little while ago. If Floyd and Russ hadn't been in jail, then he wouldn't have been there trying to get them out. He wouldn't have shot Wills.

He remembered with a cramping feeling of nausea the way the shotgun had taken Chet's chest out, the way the second blast had all but severed his head. He reined his horse off away from the others and swung limply to the ground. He bent double and threw up, gagging helplessly even after his stomach had been emptied on the ground.

He could blame Floyd for the fact that he had been in town. But the law wasn't going to blame Floyd for Chet Wills's death. The law was going to blame him. That meant he had to run. If he stayed here he would get hung.

Running meant leaving his wife and kids. He faced the future with bleak hopelessness. He'd be running all the rest of his life, he thought. He'd be running until he died. He wouldn't ever see Hannah again. He wouldn't see the kids. He'd live and die alone, and if he stayed with Floyd and Russ, they'd be outlaws, all three of them. They'd never been able to more than scratch out a bare living even when they weren't wanted by the law and there was no reason to think that was going to change.

Besides, he had the uneasy feeling that Floyd liked killing. Floyd liked thieving, believing it to be the only way he could have the things other people had. Floyd had showed no sign of shock at the sight of Chet Wills's blood and flesh blown all over the wall of the sheriff's office. He'd showed no kind of feeling at all as he came out of his cell and looked at Chet's body on the floor.

Out of the darkness came Floyd's harsh voice, "Theron? What the hell's the matter with you?"

"Nothin'. I'm comin'." Theron mounted unsteadily and guided his horse toward the sound of Floyd's voice.

Eleven men were here, counting him. Two, Floyd and Russ, were guilty of the sheriff's and Kirby's deaths. He and the rest were guilty of Chet Wills's death. That was what the law said. Everybody who was present at the time of a killing was as guilty as the man who pulled the trigger. At least they were if, at the time, they were committing a crime. And breaking prisoners out of jail was certainly a crime.

Floyd waited until he had caught up. He let Theron range up alongside and then he said, "What the hell's the matter with you?"

Anger touched Theron's voice. "What the hell do you think? I just blew Chet Wills's head off and it's the first man I ever killed."

Floyd snorted. "You and Russ are just alike. No stomach. But that'll change."

"Maybe not. Maybe I'll just stay here and take what's coming to me."

Floyd laughed sarcastically. "Sure you will. You know what they'll do to you, don't you?"

"I might not hang." The word on his own lips made him feel sick again. In his mind he could see himself mounting the scaffold steps toward the gently swinging noose at the top. He could feel the black hood put over his head, could feel the scratchy harshness of the hangman's noose as they settled it over his head and tightened it. He'd seen a hanging once. There was a big coil of rope on the hangman's noose and that, when the trapdoor was sprung, broke your neck and kept you from choking to death. As if it was yesterday he remembered the awful sound the trapdoor had made, the following sound as the body hit the end of the rope and snapped it taut with a dull kind of twang.

Floyd said, "What the hell makes you think you might not hang? When did anybody in town ever have any use for anyone named Stotts? And the people in town are the ones that will be on your jury."

"Maybe some of our friends will be on it too."

Floyd laughed harshly once more. "Friends! You think we got any friends? The only reason they're ridin' with us is greed! They want some of the Pool's land just the same as us. They don't give a damn for you an' me. They'd kill us theirselves if they thought they could get somethin' out of it."

"Then what are we goin' to do?"

"We're goin' over an' take Indian Springs. We're goin' to move ever'thing, lock, stock, and barrel, women an' kids an' ever'thin'."

"In the middle of winter?"

"They can do it. They can put up shacks that'll do until somethin' better can be built."

"And then what? We can't stay. Not you or Russ or me."

"We'll skedaddle. Before that bunch in town gets organized."

"What if they're already organized?"

"They ain't. The sheriff an' deputy are dead. Foxworthy, the son-of-a-bitch, is shot in the leg. He ain't goin' to be ridin' for a while."

Hope touched Theron. "Where are we goin' to go?"

"Hell, I don't know. We'll just ride out. Maybe we'll head up Denver way. Maybe we'll go to Pueblo. Or hell, how about Leadville? That's where we was headed with that bunch of steers. There's money to be had in Leadville, if you're tough an' hard enough."

"And you think you are, is that it? Just because you shot Ray Owens and Tom Kirby when they wasn't expectin' it?"

"You ain't no better."

"No? At least what I done was self-defense."

"That ain't what a judge an' jury is goin' to say."

Theron knew that was true. He knew, furthermore, that there was no way but Floyd's way. He couldn't surrender himself because if he did, he would hang and that was a sight worse than being an outlaw.

He asked, "What about Hal and Sam?"

"They stay. At Indian Springs. We send 'em money to stock the place. Then, someday, when there's money enough, we come back an' fight the thing."

Theron felt a touch of hope, even though he knew Floyd was fooling himself. There would be no coming back. There would be no clearing themselves, because by the time there was money for it, there would be other crimes to answer for.

But he was helpless. He had no choice. Glumly he said, "All right," and followed Floyd and Russ, who rode beside him, toward home.

CHAPTER 19

No matter how Foxworthy sat his saddle, his leg continued to throb painfully. He tried keeping it out of the stirrup, keeping the weight off it. He tried letting it hang. But nothing worked.

Furthermore, it had begun to bleed again, enough so that both bandage and trouser leg were soaked.

Alternately walking and loping, avoiding the trot because of its jolting motion, they reached Indian Springs just after sunup.

At this time of year, there was little warmth in the sun. Today it filtered through thin clouds lying close to the horizon, a huge, orange ball, looking more like a rising moon than a rising sun.

There were two men at Indian Springs, the same two Foxworthy had left there several days ago. Red Elder and Dutch Franz. They had a fire going and they had a big pile of firewood they had apparently dragged here from somewhere. They also had apparently gotten some whiskey someplace, because both were red-eyed, and they hastily tried to hide several empty bottles in the ashes of the shack as Foxworthy and the others came riding down into the bowl.

Foxworthy pretended not to notice either the way they looked or the bottles they had hidden. He'd left them here without relief a lot longer than he had intended. They'd run out of firewood and food and he couldn't blame them for going after more. He assumed only one of them had left at a time, the other staying behind to guard against attack.

Red was sheepish and seemed to have a compulsion to confess. As Dan dismounted, he said, "One of us was here all the time, Mr. Foxworthy. But we had to have a fire, an' we had to have more grub."

Foxworthy nodded. "It's all right."

Red looked surprised at his mild reply. He asked, "What are you all doin' here?"

"I figure the Stottses and their friends are on their way."

"I hear Owens and Kirby are dead."

"Where did you hear that?"

Red stammered, "I . . . we . . . Oh hell, I heard it in town when I went in for grub."

Foxworthy said, "Chet Wills is dead too. Theron Stotts killed him last night breaking Floyd and Russ out of jail."

"What makes you think that they'll come here?"

"They'll come. Floyd has got to have something to show for all that has gone wrong."

The men had dismounted and were now gathered around the fire. Foxworthy stared up toward the rim of the bowl, realizing that without cover this position was indefensible. The rim of the bowl was within rifle range of its center. Men could lie up there and shoot the defenders like targets in a shooting gallery.

Floyd, Russ, and Theron had killed before and would not hesitate to kill again. The penalty for several killings was no heavier than the penalty for one. Nor could Foxworthy's men dig in. The only defense, therefore, would be a charge when the small ranchers opened fire from the rim of the bowl and in that kind of operation men were going to get hurt and killed.

Foxworthy knew that he had no right to permit men to

be killed on both sides fighting a fight that was essentially between the Cheyenne Pool, which didn't give a damn anymore, and the Stotts family, several members of which were wanted murderers. There had to be a better way.

He yelled, "Listen! I've got something to say!"

The men at the fire turned. Foxworthy said, "I'm going to scout around. If that bunch shows up, let 'em have the springs. Pull back, stay together, and just keep an eye on them."

The men stared at him surprisedly. One of them yelled, "What about them killers? You just goin' to let 'em get away?"

"No. They won't get away. But there's no sense in more men getting killed over something that's not worth fighting for."

"You mean Indian Springs?"

"I mean all the land that's been held by the Cheyenne Pool. They're ready to quit. All they want is to run their cattle here until next fall, when they can be sold for a decent price."

He turned and limped to his horse. With difficulty he swung to the saddle. The effort left him weak and sweating and he wondered if he had the strength for what he now meant to do. He said casually, "I'll be back," and rode away in the direction of the Stotts place.

At the rim of the bowl, he halted his horse and looked around. The men were still clustered around the fire. A couple had dug bottles out of their saddlebags and were passing them around.

Wryly, Foxworthy marveled at the change that had taken place within himself in little more than a week. A week ago, he'd have led that bunch down there straight to the Stotts' place. He'd have taken Floyd and Russ and

Theron no matter who got hurt. He'd have held Indian Springs and all the other springs against everything they threw at him.

He supposed a lot of things were responsible for his change of heart. Finding Owens and Kirby buried like a couple of dogs had undoubtedly been one of them, because he had to blame himself for the two men's deaths. Floyd Stotts had to be crazy to attack the Pool, steal their cattle, and kill when he got caught. But the fact remained that his own killing of the calf in the Stotts yard had precipitated Floyd's insanity. Without that act, none of the three tragedies would probably ever have occurred.

So, being responsible, it was now his responsibility to set things right. Before more men were killed on both sides. The commissioners had appointed him to fill out Ray Owens' term and it was up to him to do it as nearly the way Ray would have done it as possible.

Ray wouldn't have led an army out here. That was what he had realized a few minutes before down there at the springs. Ray had gone after the rustlers with only Tom Kirby when he could just as easily have raised a posse and gone after them in force. He had done so to avoid bloodshed. That he hadn't succeeded wasn't due to faulty planning on his part. It was due to Floyd Stotts' sudden insanity, born of years of frustrated greed, of grinding poverty in the face of so much plenty just a few miles north of him.

Perhaps his own plan would turn out no better than Ray's had, because, like Ray, he was dealing with Floyd Stotts and Floyd's insanity. But, like Ray, he had to try. If he failed, then someone else would lead out a force to capture Floyd and Theron and Russ.

He kept his horse at a steady walk to save his leg. Once, he pulled his rifle from the boot and checked its loads.

After that he checked his revolver and slid it back loosely into its holster.

He thought of Lutie Mathias and briefly wondered if he would ever see her again. He called himself maudlin, but he knew how close death was to him.

For no particular reason, he suddenly remembered his father and mother and today, for the first time in his life he felt compassion for them. His father must have been a lot like Floyd Stotts, he thought, just half a step ahead of starvation all the time. Small wonder there had been no time for love in the Foxworthy house. There had only been time for work, and worry and the desperate terror that only people so close to starvation know.

His early life had warped his own attitudes toward life. But perhaps he could now change all that. Understanding Floyd had brought some understanding of his father. And perhaps when he better understood his father he could more thoroughly understand himself.

A mile from Indian Springs he sighted them, coming across the rolling prairie toward him. He stopped his horse on the top of a knoll and waited, watching them approach.

Floyd Stotts saw the lone horseman ahead without recognizing him at first because the distance was too great.

None of the old arrogance in bearing was apparent in Foxworthy so it was not until they had closed the distance to a quarter mile that Floyd recognized his old enemy.

Doing so brought a fierce exultation to him. He could, he told himself gleefully, kill Foxworthy today. He could kill him without penalty and hating him the way he did, he would be a fool if he didn't try.

Beside him, Theron asked, "What the hell is he doing? It looks like the son-of-a-bitch is all alone!"

That would be too much to expect, thought Floyd. No. Foxworthy was on a knoll. He probably had twenty men behind him in the draw.

Briefly, he debated the courses open to him. What he ought to do, he admitted, was to give up Indian Springs. If Foxworthy and twenty men stood in the way, it was doubtful if it could be taken anyway.

By going on, he risked capture. And if he was captured, his fate was inevitable. He would hang. So would Russ and so would Theron. Those who had been with Theron in the jail break would get prison sentences.

The smart thing to do, then, would be to turn tail and run. Their horses were at least as fresh as those of Foxworthy and his men. If they could stay out in front until darkness fell, they could probably get away.

Yet the sight of his enemy sitting his horse on that knoll alone was too tempting to Floyd. So was the thought of Indian Springs, which controlled enough range so that his family and the families of his brothers would never need to live in poverty again.

The others had halted behind him. Now they shifted uneasily in their saddles. One of the men who had been in on the jail break asked, "What the hell are we waitin' for? Let's get the hell out of here!"

Floyd said, "Wait. Maybe he's all alone."

A man behind him laughed bitterly. "No chance. Foxworthy may be a lot of things, but he ain't no goddam fool."

Floyd asked, "How do we know how many men he's got?"

"We know he's got enough to beat the hell out of us or he wouldn't be sittin' there."

"Then why don't they show themselves?"

"He don't want us to know how many of 'em he's got."

Floyd said, "That don't make no sense. If he wanted to lure us into a trap, he'd show us just enough to make us think we had a chance. Wouldn't he?"

The man wavered. "Maybe. But then why's he sittin' there all alone?"

Floyd said, "Why don't we go and see?"

A man in the rear of the group said, "Not me!"

Floyd swung around savagely. "You were in on that jailbreak, Jake. I saw you there. You're guilty of murder just the same as Theron is. You want to go home and sit there waitin' for them to come take you in? You ever thought what a rope feels like when they put it around your neck? You ever seen a man hit the end of that rope when they spring the trap?"

Jake didn't answer him. Floyd said, "Come on, then. Let's see what the son-of-a-bitch has got in mind."

He kicked his horse in the ribs and the animal forged ahead. Both doubtfully and fearfully, his men followed him. At a steady walk, they approached the solitary figure of Foxworthy on the hill.

Foxworthy didn't move. He made no move toward his gun. His rifle remained in the saddle boot.

Uneasily, Floyd stared at him. The bastard had to have something up his sleeve or he wouldn't be sitting there as if he owned the world.

He wished he could see beyond Foxworthy and into the draw. But he could not and he had chosen his course and now was committed to it. Once more, face was an important factor. If he backed off now, he would lose face with his family. And he had already lost too much.

Besides, he told himself, if he kept on, he'd get a chance to kill Foxworthy. No matter how many men were in the draw, he'd get a chance to kill his enemy before they could move, before they could do a thing.

He kicked his horse in the ribs and the animal broke into a trot. On Floyd's face was an expression of gleeful anticipation, because in his mind Foxworthy was already lying dead. All that was needed was to put a bullet into him, and at this range, it was practically a certainty. Floyd let his hand caress the receiver of his rifle, which he knew was cocked and had a cartridge in the chamber. A few more yards, he thought. A few more yards . . .

CHAPTER 20

When Floyd and those with him were still fifty yards away, Foxworthy raised both hands, palms outward to show their emptiness. He shouted, "Hold it! I want to talk!" He had deliberately taken his stand on this knoll, knowing they would suspect that he had reinforcements in the draw behind.

Floyd halted, his rifle in his hands. The others halted too. Foxworthy shouted, "I've been appointed by the commissioners to take Ray Owens's place!"

Those with Floyd looked at one another, plainly trying to figure this out. Foxworthy shouted, "And I'm not working for the Pool any more!"

Floyd bawled, "Then what about Indian Springs? You going to give it up?"

"How can I? I'm not working for the Pool any more."

Floyd turned his head. "What are we listening to this bastard for? Let's go!"

Foxworthy shouted, "It's not going to be that easy. I've got warrants for you and Russ and Theron and for everyone that was in on that jailbreak the other night! The charge is murder!"

Floyd yelled, "Come take us then, you son-of-a-bitch!"

Foxworthy raised his voice, knowing he now had very little time. "The rest of you can ride away! I just want Floyd and Russ and Theron! I don't give a damn about the other warrants! I'll even tear them up! But by God, if you stand back of Floyd, you'll hang right along with him! Or spend the rest of your lives down at the pen!"

A man yelled, "What about the Springs?"

Anger now touched Foxworthy. "I'm not talking about land! I'm talking about your lives! Fight with Floyd now and you'll hang with him!"

"But what about the Springs?"

Foxworthy shrugged resignedly. "All right! The Pool is folding up. They've got to keep their cattle on that land until next fall so they can sell out at a decent price, but after that it's up for grabs!"

He could almost see the greed working in their minds. And it didn't take Floyd long to realize that the ground was being cut out from under him. He roared, "Don't listen to that lyin' bastard! He's still workin' for the Pool and he ain't about to give up any land! All he wants to do is split us apart!"

Foxworthy gambled now. He roared, "Hell, I've got enough men with me to take all of you! And you've got just one damn minute to make up your minds!"

Floyd looked around at the faces of the other men. Turning back, he flung his rifle to his shoulder furiously. He fired, but a horse reined suddenly against his own, spoiled his aim and the bullet missed.

Foxworthy didn't dare to try and defend himself. He shouted, "Make up your minds! You ain't got all day!"

Floyd was scuffling now with the man who had jostled his horse. Someone in the group with Floyd yelled, "Give the warrants to us! Let us tear them up ourselves!"

Foxworthy pulled the warrants out and flung them toward the men. "That's all right with me!"

Before anybody could dismount and pick them up, Floyd slammed his rifle stock into the face of the man with whom he was scuffling. He reined his horse away, face livid with fury. "You lousy bunch of yellow-bellies! Come on, Russ! You too, Theron!" His brothers joined him and the three pulled away. They turned their horses and faced Foxworthy and the group defiantly.

Foxworthy felt a surge of triumph. Through a combination of threats and an appeal to their greed, he had succeeded in splitting them. Floyd, Russ, and Theron were now on one side, Sam and Hal Stotts on the other.

The same man's voice yelled, "We ain't goin' to help you, though! You're on your own!"

Floyd bawled furiously, "Stupid! You're playin' the bastard's game!"

The man replied, "Maybe. But we ain't killers an' you three are."

Floyd swung his rifle and fired instantly. The man was driven off his horse. He fell spread-eagled on the ground and afterward laid still.

Foxworthy didn't wait. He yelled, "Now you can see what a rattlesnake he is!"

Hal Stotts shouted, "All right! Come get 'em! You'll get 'em anyhow an' the rest of us had just as well save our necks! We wasn't in on those killin's. We didn't have nothin' to do with 'em!"

The group reined away, turning back toward town, leaving Floyd, Russ and Theron sitting their horses all alone.

Foxworthy yanked his rifle from the boot. He jacked a cartridge in. He'd been fearful of drawing the gun before, but he wasn't now. No longer did he have more than a dozen men to face. Now there were only three.

Only three? Maybe he had succeeded in avoiding an all-out war between his own posse and this group. He had confronted Floyd's bunch and he was still alive. But he hadn't captured the three murderers and the way things stood, he wasn't sure he could. He bawled, "Hold it, Floyd! I'll shoot if you raise that gun!"

Floyd's gun came up, firing the instant it was level. But he had fired too hastily and his bullet missed. With an awareness of the odds against him, Foxworthy also fired too hastily. The bullet intended for Floyd struck Russ instead, knocking him off his horse, which spooked and ran, dragging Russ, whose foot caught in the stirrup as he fell. Several of the men who had ridden away toward town turned and spurred their mounts after the runaway, but Foxworthy didn't take time to see whether they caught up with him or not. He was watching Floyd, and Theron, who both were armed and still very dangerous.

He'd cut the odds but he wasn't in the clear. Floyd spurred his horse suddenly toward Foxworthy's left. At the same instant, Theron spurred his horse to Foxworthy's right.

Split, they circled him on opposite sides, wanting him in a crossfire, wanting to force him to divide his attention between the two of them.

Foxworthy knew Floyd was the most dangerous. He also knew Floyd would be the hardest of the two to hit. His decision made, he reined his horse to the right and sank his spurs.

The animal leaped into motion with a jerk that nearly unseated him. Pain from his wounded leg seemed to shoot clear to his brain. But the horse was in motion now, and behind him Foxworthy heard Floyd's roar of fury, also heard the volley of shots Floyd pumped from his gun.

Leaning low over his horse's withers, Dan raced straight toward Theron who, taken by surprise, was momentarily motionless.

Too late, Theron tried to turn his horse out of the way.

Seeing that would fail, he brought his rifle up, lining it and firing it almost in Foxworthy's face.

Foxworthy felt the hot blast from its muzzle. The concussion nearly deafened him. Something stung his ear, but then he was on Theron, swinging his rifle savagely. The muzzle struck Theron on the side of the head with a sharply audible crack.

Theron's rifle went flying. He stayed in the saddle for an instant. Then, as his horse shied away in fright, he toppled to one side and slid out of it to the ground.

Foxworthy reined his horse around so sharply that the animal reared. Rearing, he caught, in his chest the bullet that had been aimed at his rider. The sound of it striking was unmistakable and instead of coming down on all four feet, the horse went over backward helplessly.

Foxworthy, caught unawares, tried to leap clear. He almost made it, but not quite. The horse fell on his wounded leg, and the pain was so terrible, so burning, that for a moment he lost consciousness.

He came to an instant later with his head whirling, with the knowledge in him that Floyd had escaped. He shook his head angrily to clear it.

He still held his rifle. The horse was still, his weight pinning his wounded leg to the ground.

He had not the strength to pull it clear and he knew if he tried the pain would make him lose consciousness again.

He'd thought that Floyd would be long gone, but Floyd was not. He could have escaped, but his hatred for Foxworthy was too great. He was coming, his rifle held at shoulder height, ready to shoot the moment he was sure of his kill.

Foxworthy couldn't remember whether he had a live shell in the chamber of the rifle or not. He knew he didn't dare take the chance that he did, yet he also knew that while he was working the lever to pump a fresh cartridge in, Floyd would aim his gun and shoot.

Frantically Foxworthy tried to recall whether or not he'd jacked another cartridge in after shooting Russ. He couldn't remember to save his life and, he realized wryly, that was exactly what depended on his remembering.

But he always jacked a cartridge in after firing. It was automatic, reflex.

Floyd now was close enough. Deliberately he raised his gun, put the gun to his shoulder, sighting it on Foxworthy's chest.

Foxworthy raised his own rifle. His decision had been made. If the gun was loaded he had a chance. If it was not, he was a man already dead. He squeezed the trigger as the gun came in line.

Floyd had thought his enemy was helpless. He had thought all he had to do was finish him off. Seeing Foxworthy conscious, seeing him raise his gun, probably affected his aim.

Both guns fired simultaneously. Foxworthy's slug struck Floyd squarely in the chest, tearing into bone and flesh, spreading the way a lead bullet will, and making a jagged tear as it went on through. Its force was terrible at this range and it flung Floyd back as though he had been struck by a giant fist. His body jerked, and he sat down hard, his eyes already glazed.

Floyd's bullet tore a ragged furrow in the dirt three feet behind Foxworthy and ricocheted off, whining, into space. Foxworthy laid the rifle down. He put his hands against the horse's body, and pulled against his imprisoned leg.

Lights flashed before his eyes. The pain was dizzying. But he budged the leg. An inch. Two. He didn't know.

Placing his hands against the horse again, he pulled again. Floyd was dead, and Russ was probably dead also. But Theron was only knocked out by the blow of the rifle barrel and might be regaining consciousness at any time.

Again he pulled, and again budged the leg only an inch or two. Had not the ground been soft and dry here on the crest of the knoll, he could not have moved it at all. He pulled again, getting a little frantic, and though the pain nearly overcame him, at last he felt the leg come free.

Using the rifle as a crutch, he forced himself to his feet. He stared toward Theron, who was stirring now.

Looking beyond, he saw that Hal and Sam and the others had caught and freed Russ from the stirrup. Apparently Russ's wound was superficial, because he was standing, supported between two of his friends.

But Floyd was dead. He lay on his back, staring with wide-open, sightless eyes at the sky.

Foxworthy looked back toward Indian Springs, relieved to see the posse coming at full gallop.

He turned and sat down wearily on the body of his horse. It was over, he thought. It was over, and he was alive.

He thought of Lutie Mathias, and thought of her promise to him. He let himself be boosted upon a horse. He rode out, alone, toward town, knowing both his weakness and his pain would pass. A different man than he had been a week ago, he decided he liked the new man better than the old.

OIL CITY LIBRARY
Patten, Lewis B.
The Cheyenne Pool
WEST PAT

3 3535 00072 9943